# Hard Rock

# RUTH DOWLEY

Andersen Press • London

*To David*
*with love*

First published in 2006 by
Andersen Press Limited,
20 Vauxhall Bridge Road, London SW1V 2SA
www.andersenpress.co.uk

British Library Cataloguing in Publication Data available

ISBN-10: 1 84270 467 2
ISBN-13: 978 1 84270 467 7

Typeset by FiSH Books, Enfield, Middx.
Printed and bound in Great Britain by
Bookmarque Ltd.,
Croydon, Surrey

# 1

I found the witched woman the year things got really bad. Dad was being pathetic, and I hated Gilly. The week we were on holiday, I lost it.

We rented this nowhere cottage. Gilly saw the ad. 'Away from it all,' she read out. 'Unspoilt coast three minutes from the door.'

'Boring,' I said.

Naturally, she paid no attention.

When we arrived, Dad and I carried stuff in from the car. Gilly fussed around wiping the kitchen. She has a thing about germs.

It was a done-up fisherman's cottage, grey stone with new PVC windows that Gilly bewailed as *such a pity*. Downstairs was all together, kitchen one side and sitting room the other. Shells and stones spread over shelves and drift wood curled around the fireplace like the sea had washed in.

Arthur started examining the shells straight away. 'This big crinkly one opens. Look, Mummy.'

Gilly turned from sniffing in the fridge. 'That's a scallop. You don't often see both halves together. A little creature lived in there.' She was always pleased to impart educational information. You felt you were being crammed for an exam.

Arthur made the shell open and close at me as I

heaved a cardboard box onto the counter. 'Hi yuh, hi yuh!' he squeaked.

'Where do these bags go?' puffed Dad.

Decide yourself, I thought, but he was too well trained.

'By the stairs for now,' said Gilly. She glanced towards me. 'And put that box by the sink. I'm just going to wipe there.'

I pretended not to hear. Humping the flipping thing from the boot nearly killed me. Jars were cunningly hidden under muesli and bread.

'Les!' she demanded. 'By the sink, please.'

'Les*lie*,' I corrected. 'Why can't you move it? It's only two steps.'

'Because I asked you.'

'Come on now,' said Dad. 'Be helpful.'

'I *am*!'

He put on his cheery, pretend-we're-happy voice. 'As soon as we get sorted, we can go to the beach.'

Gilly shoved a hand on her hip and looked down at me. She's almost as tall as Dad. 'I'm waiting,' she said.

I grabbed the carton and dumped it by the sink. Glass smacked together.

'Thank *you*.' She checked to see if anything had broken.

Dad pulled my head against him and said quietly, 'Lighten up, sweetheart.'

'You're smothering me.' I butted him off, but not hard.

'Sa-mothering, sa-mothering,' sang Arthur. 'What's smothering?'

'Can't breathe,' said Gilly.

Arthur screwed up his face.

When things were arranged as it pleased her majesty, we went upstairs to put on our swimsuits under our clothes. My room was the size of a cupboard. You couldn't even open the bottom drawer of the chest. It was wedged sideways between the bed and the outside wall.

Arthur had a bigger room, because Gilly said he could play with his cars and stuff on the floor in the morning. She was strict about him not waking her and Dad when they were sleeping in. Supposedly. Sometimes they were definitely not sleeping. I wanted to bang their door and tell them to get up and look after Arthur.

I heard him jumping on the creaky bunk bed in his room, refusing to change. Gilly's voice came through the thin excuse of a partition wall next to my bed. 'You'll only be able to paddle in your shorts. It's *such* fun in the sea. We can jump waves!'

'Don't want to,' said Arthur. She had organised him into swimming lessons especially for this holiday, but he didn't like them.

'I'll take your suit and armbands in case you change your mind. Now pop into the lavatory before we go.'

She pushed my door open without knocking. "Take something warm to put on after swimming. Arthur's in the bathroom, but there's another lavatory downstairs if you want one.'

3

'I don't need you to tell me when *to wee*!'

She clicked on martyr mode. 'I was only being helpful.'

That'll be the day, I thought.

In the kitchen, she doled out more stuff to carry. The bags I got were crammed so full, the handles hardly reached across the top. They were heavy as sacks of bricks. One contained a two-litre bottle of mineral water. 'I'm going to develop gorilla biceps at this rate,' I groaned.

Gilly clutched her throat dramatically. 'My necklace!'

We looked to see what had happened to it, but of course nothing had.

It was *the* necklace. I was younger than Arthur the first time I saw it. Gilly had been reading to me while she and Dad waited for Shushy to come and baby-sit. Probably *Snow White*. It should have been anyway.

Something tickled my hair. A delicate golden chain swung above, each link made of tiny swirls. I reached up with a fingertip. 'I love that!'

'Isn't it beautiful?' Gilly gushed. 'Your daddy gave it to me.'

The shining links trembled in the lamplight. I'd never seen anything so wonderful. Why hadn't he given it to me? I'd have treasured it. I wanted to snatch it off her.

'That's enough story,' I said and got down from her lap. I snatched my book away instead of the necklace.

'Say thank you, there's a good girl,' said Dad. 'Where are you going?'

I didn't answer.

'Want a different story?' called Gilly. 'Bring me one.'

But I marched to my room and sat on the floor, biting the corner of *Snow White* or equivalent. The necklace went on trembling in an empty, hurting place I had inside me. I was angry at Gilly which was fine, but I was also angry at Dad which was scary.

In the living room, Gilly prattled on in her awful flirty voice as if I'd stopped existing. Dad laughed. Then two certainties hit me, hit me so hard that I bit a dent into the corner of my book.

*The necklace should have been my mother's.*

And *Daddy was going to marry Gilly.*

Now we bunched up around Gilly and the necklace at the cottage door. Dad said, 'I don't think salt water will hurt gold.'

Gilly reached under her immaculately arranged hair and undid it. 'A link could snap while I'm swimming. I'd be *devastated*! I'd better leave it.'

'Put it in the crinkly shell,' said Arthur. He pulled a tissue from the box she'd efficiently placed on the side table. He folded it into the bottom of the shell. 'Make a nest.'

Gilly let him curl the necklace on the tissue. He knelt on the sofa and carefully balanced the closed shell on the shelf behind. 'Now it's got something living in it again.'

On the lane, a fresh-smelling salty breeze slid past my face. Gulls dipped overhead, calling hello. It was good to be out, even lugging the monster bags.

Arthur skipped beside me, clutching his bucket and two spades. 'Will you help build a sand castle?'

'Maybe.' I would, but I didn't want Gilly to hear me say so. I wasn't doing it to please her.

She butted in from behind anyway. 'I warned you there might not be much sand on our little beach.'

Arthur drooped.

'Real castles weren't made with sand,' I said. 'You could build one with stones.'

'Yeah, that's *better*! Let's do stones! Stony, stony stones!'

Another old cottage squatted at the end of the lane. As we approached, music swirled around us.

'Listen,' said Dad. 'Hear what instrument that is, Arthur?'

'Violin,' said Arthur. He'd have to be a complete dork not to know. Gilly's had him taking violin lessons since he was three. I ask you.

'Right!' exclaimed Dad, revving up fake enthusiasm. 'That family must like violin music too.'

'Am I in this family?' I muttered.

Arthur is supposed to listen to recordings of his new pieces a million times. Gilly had *Perpetual Motion* driving me perpetually bonkers on the journey down, until I told her that any more motion would make me car sick. She stops if I make a remark. She's scared I'll put him off.

A dirt track led on from the lane between gorse and brambles. Arthur kept jumping up, demanding, 'I want to see the sea!' I couldn't see it either, though the music behind us drowned under pounding that had to be breakers.

Then, abruptly, we were on a cliff edge. I stared into vast water and sky. They hardly separated on the long blue-grey horizon. The great round of air before us was enough to fill the lungs of all the creatures on earth. Along the coast, ridges of broken cliff sped down and jutted into the sea. Foaming waves crashed over their rocky feet and leaped against outcrops.

How can I explain what happened? The rocks and sea and sky *claimed* me. Like I was supposed to have come. Like I was meant to be here, right here, now.

Below us, boulders barricaded each side of a small cove. A path snaked steeply down the cliff. Hummocks of rough grass edged the drop.

'Better hold my hand,' Gilly said to Arthur.

'I don't need to.'

'Go in front then, Chris,' she told Dad.

I was already going down first. Dad was loaded with bags, the blanket, and the wind shield. 'Leslie's there,' he said.

Arthur leaned two hands on my back. 'You're the engine. I'm the carriage.'

My foot skidded. 'Runaway train!' I said. 'Brake!' Arthur screeched.

'What's the matter?' yelled Gilly.

'Train braking!' Arthur shouted.

'Don't mess about, either of you. We don't want to start the holiday with an accident.'

7

No, let's just keep on with the nagging. Some get away from it all. How was I going to survive eight days of undiluted Gilly?

I looked at the rocks. Along there. I'll get away along there so far you'll never find me.

Just then, two people climbed over the boulders edging the beach. A girl with a pony tail sticking out of the back of a cap and a cool-looking boy.

They jumped down and scrunched across the shingle towards us.

# 2

With no one else on the beach, we were bound to speak. The girl looked younger than me and the boy maybe older. His copper-coloured hair flopped around freckles and gorgeous big sparkly eyes. They both smiled.

'Bet you're in the other holiday cottage,' the girl said.

'The second one up the lane? Yeah.' I smiled back, especially at the boy.

'Well, isn't that nice!' Gilly exclaimed, shoving in. She took over introductions.

I shut up. I didn't want to be part of her scene. But I made sure I got their names. Simon and Kate.

'We heard music coming from your cottage,' Dad said.

'Mum,' said Kate. 'Practising.' She rolled her eyes.

'That was *your mum* playing?' cried Gilly.

'She's in an orchestra,' Simon said.

'Did you hear, Arthur? That violin was live! Arthur plays the violin.'

Simon grinned at Arthur. 'Suzuki? Great.' He flashed a smile at Kate that made her laugh.

Arthur leaned against me and studied them. 'We're going to build a stone castle. Real ones aren't sand. Want to help?'

I thought they wouldn't want to play with a little kid who wasn't even their brother, but Simon said, 'Sounds a great excuse to put off swimming. It's freezing.'

Dad glanced uneasily at the waves. 'Is it?'

'We've given up rock climbing. The tide's coming in,' Kate said.

'How *sensible*,' said Gilly. 'One can't be too careful with tides.'

She made me want to scream. I dumped the bags. 'Come on,' I told Arthur.

I hoped Simon and Kate would follow, and they did. The four of us skidded down the shingle. Near the water's edge, patches of gritty sand lay between pebbles and seaweed. We started skimming stones. Kate hopped one five times.

'Brilliant!' yelled Simon.

'Skill,' Kate said, tugging the brim of her cap.

I found flat pebbles for Arthur. I tried to show him how to flick his wrist, but they splashed straight in.

'Oh, plop!' he cried after the third one.

Simon hurled a stone into the wash of a wave. 'Double plop! See who makes the biggest splash.' He grinned at me.

I crashed a stone in too. Kate threw one sideways. It splattered us. Arthur chuckled. He heaved up a rock with both hands, chucked it into the next wave and jumped away. Water shot over Simon's legs. Kate whooped.

Simon hit the beach as if he'd been knocked backwards. 'You pack some power, kid!' He was so *nice*!

'This castle,' said Kate, 'shall we make it below the tide line?'

'What's it going to be tied with?' asked Arthur.

'Sea tide,' I said. 'Below the place the sea stops coming in.'

'Will it all-fall-down?'

'It'll be more exciting if water gets round it,' said Kate.

Arthur looked uncertain, but she adjusted her cap and marked a circle in the gritty sand.

We pulled off our trainers. Gilly hurried to collect mine and Arthur's. She'd made Dad pound in the wind shield by a boulder higher up and smoothed a place for the blanket.

She felt the water. 'Oh, this is fine,' she declared. 'But you build your castle first.' As if we needed her permission!

She went back to her camp with a smug expression that said, Look how well I'm organising it so they can have fun. Dad was punching a number into his mobile.

'You're not phoning the office, are you?' said Gilly.

'Just checking a couple of things.'

'We've just got on *the beach*! Put it away!'

Dad smiled sheepishly, holding the mobile to his ear. 'Doesn't seem to be a signal.'

He lay down, arms folded on his chest. She tickled him. He caught her hand and kissed it. I blocked them out.

'O-*K,*' said Kate. 'First lay a foundation. Big flat stones. About four wide.'

As the wall grew, she and Simon knew how to turn

the occasional stone upright to support the others. We stuffed the gaps with pebbles and seaweed.

Some of the pebbles were fantastic. Striped or speckled or odd-shaped. I held one out. 'Looks like an egg.'

Kate picked up a smooth pale hump. 'Vanilla ice-cream. Want a lick?'

'Yum,' said Arthur, 'I *love* ice-cream, but some kinds have bad stuff in them.'

Gilly is a maniac about additives and preservatives. Not that I want my insides pickled. I just hate the lectures.

'Your egg's sandstone,' said Simon. 'And the ice-cream's a kind of quartz.'

'What's this little one like a throat sweet?' asked Arthur.

'Probably purple jasper.'

I was impressed. Nice *and* clever.

Arthur put the jasper stone in his pocket.

Kate leaned over and fitted her vanilla ice-cream into Simon's section of wall. They seemed so friendly together. If my mum had gone on being in our family, Arthur might have been near my age. Well, not Arthur because, poor kid, he was half Gilly's. But I could have a cool friend of a brother like Simon.

By half a metre high, the walls narrowed to single stone thickness. Bits started to fall off. The tide was creeping up, so we dug the moat.

'We need a flag pole to finish it off,' said Simon.

We hunted along the cliff bottom. Gilly looked up from her book and smiled beatifically as we passed.

Kate kicked a plastic cup with a sandwich wrapper sticking out. 'Some people are slobs, aren't they?'

I pulled up the end of a driftwood stick. My fingers slid along its smooth curves. 'Here.'

'Perfect,' said Simon. His eyes rested on it like he saw how beautiful it was too.

'What about a flag?' said Kate. 'The towels are too big.'

Arthur scampered to the blanket. 'Can I have my swimming trunks?'

Gilly beamed and dug them out. I watched her face change when he raced off and handed them to Kate. Ha!

Kate tied the waist string to the pole and stuck it in the middle of the castle. The little suit's red and yellow patches fluttered snazzily.

Gilly came down the beach with a phoney smile. 'Aren't you all clever!' she cooed. 'But wouldn't this be more the shape of a flag?' She held out one of Dad's navy socks.

'Too boring,' said Arthur.

'But we're going in the water now. Come on! You don't want to be left out!'

She went on wheedling, but there was no chance. Dad wasn't keen either. When we went to get ready, he said, 'Think I'll just read today. Enjoy the fresh air.'

'No you won't!' Gilly threatened to tickle him again. 'You need the exercise.'

Simon ran from behind the boulder where he'd changed. He splashed straight in, high-stepping. 'Oh, oh, oh!' he winced.

Kate sploshed after him, squealing. I tested the water and pulled my foot out fast.

Dad lumbered to the edge with Gilly. His belly wobbled over the waist of his swimming trunks. It shocked me. He was *fat*.

'Want a water piggyback?' he asked Arthur with Gilly-pleasing jollity.

'Yes!' exclaimed Gilly. 'Let Daddy give you a ride.'

Arthur turned his back on them. 'I'm guarding the castle.'

Gilly squared her shoulders. 'Well, *I'm* not missing a chance to swim in the sea.' She marched in like ice was her favourite temperature and did serious swimming back and forth parallel to the shore. She's mad on keeping fit. She even does press-ups.

Dad held out his hand. 'It's you and me then, sweetheart.'

We inched in as deep as my waist. Dad exaggerated shivers. 'Be all r-r-right when we get u-used to it.' He held his nose. 'One, two, three. Belly flop!' Accurate description. He hit the water like a whale, getting me so wet there was no point not going under.

Kate swam up and tapped Dad. 'Tag! You're It!'

Dad passed It straight on to me. He wasn't very fast in the water, so I had to let him catch me a few other times, especially when Gilly pushed in and kept tagging him. It was a good game though. Simon chased me a lot.

After awhile, the sky clouded over. Waves spilled into the castle moat and slapped the wall. We got out and stood around, drying off and watching.

'Is it going to fall down?' asked Arthur.

'No way!' said Kate. 'Look at that skill building.'

Arthur crouched. 'Get back!' he made the castle scream at the waves.

'We're coming to smoother you down!' he made the waves hiss.

'No you're not! Get back!' shrieked the castle.

Dad shook his head. 'People have been saying that for hundreds of years.'

'We better go,' Simon said to Kate.

'See you tomorrow?' Kate asked me. 'We're rock climbing in the morning.'

'I was going to do that.'

'Want to go together?' asked Simon.

My heart did a little skip. 'Great.'

Arthur grabbed my arm. 'Me too, me too!'

'No, lovie,' said Gilly. 'They'll be too ambitious. I'll take you for a climb.'

'I want to go with them!' He bumped my arm with his head. 'Please, please, *please*!'

Gilly might agree, if I promised to look after him. But he'd never keep up with the others. I couldn't be held back baby-sitting when Simon *asked* me to go.

# 3

'It is going to rain,' I said after we got dressed.

Gilly went on passing out sandwiches. 'Don't be an optimist,' she said. This from the world champion neurotic.

'Look at the sky.'

But she wasn't going to lose credit for getting up at six to organise a picnic for our first day. 'It's lighter over there.'

'You mean the grey under the black cloud?'

'I could eat a supermarket of food,' said Arthur.

'You'd only be allowed to eat the healthy stuff,' I said. Dad laughed.

We'd stopped at a motorway café for lunch. Gilly had flipped when she saw Dad's plate. 'You're not having *chips*?' she said like 'You're not having arsenic?'

'I'm on holiday,' he answered.

'Your heart isn't.'

'Let him eat what he wants,' I said.

'I don't want him to have a heart attack!'

I hated her for saying that. Ever since I remembered, I'd worried about Dad having a car accident. I always said a thank you prayer when I heard his key in the door. Now I began to worry about his heart. After seeing the belly overhang, I was even more anxious. Dad ate loads of junk. He buried the wrappers at the bottom of the bin.

I'd just bitten into a pear, when it started tipping it down.

'What did I tell you?' I said.

But Gilly never admitted she was wrong. She ignored me and told us to put towels over our heads. She and Dad jammed things into bags. 'Get the blanket, Les,' she ordered.

'Leslie!' I corrected. I tried to clench the pear between my teeth while I folded, but it was too soft. I opened my mouth over a bag to drop it in. Wouldn't you know? It missed. It was a nice sweet pear too. I hope the seagulls found it.

We slogged back to the cottage and just got inside when Gilly cried, 'Arthur's swimming trunks! Did anyone fetch them?'

'They'll be there in the morning,' panted Dad.

'They won't. The tide will get them. I'll have to go back.'

Her technique for getting Dad to do something was to say she'd have to do it. Sure enough, he said, 'Give it a minute to ease, and I'll go.'

Gilly eyed me and sighed.

'It's not my fault!' I said.

'You might have thought. You were looking after the castle building.'

'You told me to bring the blanket and fifty million other things. They're *Arthur*'s trunks.'

'Little people aren't good at remembering.'

'Good reason when they're being forced into things.'

'Watch it, Les.'

'Stop calling me Les!'

Dad dabbed his face with his towel. 'What's the problem with your name all of a sudden?'

'Les is not my name.'

'It's a nickname. Like Gilly. Like Chris.'

He always took Gilly's side. I went steely. 'I want my proper name! Leslie. *The name my mother gave me.*'

Gilly froze. Dad's face crumpled. No one ever said, Don't mention your mother in front of Gilly, but I knew I wasn't supposed to.

'Mummy, I found a throat sweet on the beach,' said Arthur. 'It tastes salty.' He stuck out his tongue to show her.

'Get that out of your mouth!' Gilly screamed. She held out her hand and Arthur dropped it on. 'You must never—'

'Fooled you! It's a stone.'

Dad faked a laugh.

'You did fool me,' said Gilly, with a grudging smile. 'But, lovie, don't put stones in your mouth either. You might choke.'

'It's a casper stone,' said Arthur.

'Jasper,' I mumbled.

'How do you know?' asked Gilly.

'Simon,' said Arthur. 'And there's a kind made out of sand scrunched up tight.' He squeezed his fist.

'That's interesting. Maybe we could make a collection,' said Gilly. She frowned as a burst of rain pelted the windows. 'Somehow I don't think it's going

18

to let up. That path will be dangerously slippery soon.'

'Why did you make us come here if you're scared of people falling down cliffs?' I said. It was no thanks to her that it turned out I liked it.

'I'm on my way,' Dad said cheerily.

'Get those wet clothes off,' Gilly told me. 'You're in the shower after us. We won't be a minute.' She hustled Arthur upstairs.

Dad dropped his voice. 'You seem uptight. If you want to talk about anything...we could find a time.'

'I don't!' I sounded crosser than I meant to. I hate things being bad between me and Dad.

Why did he have to make talking to me into some special favour? I'm scheduling time for Leslie stuff. He only wanted to stop me mentioning my mother in front of boss queen. Once he told me that second wives are jealous of first wives, which is ridiculous because the second wife's got the man.

The radiator in my room wouldn't come on. Knees pressed against the cold metal, I watched Dad from the window. He did a pathetic waddling jog onto the lane, his head bent under the rain.

I should have gone. Suppose he slipped. I got this image of him bouncing down, the fat bits getting gored by sticking out rocks. Sick, I know, but it was Gilly's fault for scaring me. She should be the one out there falling on her head.

She yelled that the shower was free, but I didn't move. When I was little, I wondered why I didn't have a mother. I knew Shushy wasn't my mother. She was wrinklier than the mums who collected the others from nursery, and she went home every evening even if I wanted her to stay.

One day when I was helping her tidy, a photo fell out of a book. Dad looking skinny with his arm around a woman.

'Who's that?' I asked.

Shushy stared at the photo. 'Bless you, precious, I expect that's your mummy,' she said quietly. She gave me a squeeze and plumped a kiss on the top of my head.

My heart pounded. I had a mum!

Shushy held the book open. 'Better put it back. I expect Daddy keeps it tucked away because it makes him feel sad.'

That's when the empty hurting place first told me it was there. I felt sad too.

I got the photo out again after Dad came home. I asked him where my mummy was. He didn't tell me what happened. He cuddled me a lot and said she wasn't with us anymore, but we had each other. When I mentioned her the next day, he changed the subject. I guessed his sadness gave him an empty hurting place like mine. I tried to make it up to him by being extra good.

Before he married Gilly, Dad gave me a photo of my own. Without him in it. My mother is leaning against a tree. She's smiling sweetly. She looks gentle and kind. Dad says she was. But how could a gentle and kind person do what she did?

A few times, I called Gilly Mummy. I wanted to be like the other kids. Shushy came less and less. Gilly arranged swaps with the mothers of girls in my nursery class. I went to one of their houses until she could pick me up.

'It's nicer for you to have friends to play with,' she said.

It wasn't nicer. 'They aren't my friends,' I said.

'They soon will be,' said Gilly.

She bought me new clothes and toys, but she wasn't comfy like Shushy. I had to finish my first course before I could have pudding. I hardly ever got sweets except when Dad gave them to me on the sly. I had strict bedtimes. Worst of all, Gilly was always there when Dad was home.

I started not calling her any name. It was difficult if I needed to shout in a hurry. One day, I copied Dad and called her Gilly. I knew from the silence that she'd rather be called Mummy. I felt powerful. Tough for you, I thought. You're not my mummy!

When Dad's blurred shape appeared lumbering up the lane, I went to have my shower. Lukewarm. Gilly and Arthur must have used all the hot water. I went back to my cold cupboard room and crawled into bed with a paperback and Mum's photo.

Nobody knew I'd brought my photo. It was only a snapshot, but I had it in a frame. Before I packed it, I wrapped the frame in a T-shirt for protection. At home, the photo lived on my bedside table turned away from the light. I was scared of the colours fading.

Arthur ran along the passage. I covered the photo with my book. He burst in. He had on his fleece over his pyjamas. 'We're going to play snap. Want to?'

'I'm reading.'

'Why are you under the duvet?'

'The stupid radiator doesn't work!'

He scooted into his room and came back dragging the duvet from the spare bunk. 'I've got two. Put this one on your top part.' He tried to heave it onto the bed to wrap round me.

We smiled at each other as I pulled it up. 'Thanks,' I said. 'You're sweet.'

He skipped off downstairs. I heard him calling, 'Leslie wants to read, and her radiator's broken.'

'It's warm down here, Leslie,' Dad shouted, but he didn't come and try to fix the radiator. He and Gilly made lots of noise during snap to make me think I was missing something terrific.

After the row subsided, I went to get a drink. I thought I'd offer to read Arthur a story. But the television was on. An electric fire glowed in the grate, turning the driftwood on the floor dusky gold.

'There you are!' said Gilly.

Dad had his arm around her on the sofa. She had the necklace back on. Arthur lay with his head on her lap and his feet on Dad's. He looked at me with big sleepy eyes, sucking his thumb.

'Come and join us,' said Dad.

Why should I? They weren't missing me at all.

# 4

Gilly said we should relax and sleep in the next morning. Some hope. After it got light, Arthur's little cars were bombarding the paper wall next to my bed. I tried to get another half hour after everyone went downstairs, but it was useless. The curtains were practically transparent. The sun belted straight through onto my face.

I came down to more *Perpetual Motion*. I clutched my stomach. Gilly frowned and switched it off. Dad gave me a please-don't-cause-trouble look. It's OK for him. He's usually at work when the CDs are on. He leaves before we have breakfast and comes home when Arthur's ready for bed.

I swung my legs over the bench to sit by Arthur. He dropped his spoon in his cereal. It splattered me with milk.

'*Arthur*! What'd you do that for?'

'Sor-ry. The spoon's upset so it made an upset,' he said. 'It wants me to go rock climbing with you.'

'Well you can't.'

Gilly handed me the dishcloth. 'Be careful on those rocks, won't you? Don't take any risks.' She leaned in front of Dad and moved the margarine. 'You don't need that much.'

'I thought this kind had olive oil in it,' said Dad.

23

'Only a percentage. Do you want toast, Leslie?'

I shook my head as I rubbed the milk blobs. The Leslie gave me a second's satisfaction until she added, 'Have you got your watch? Be back by quarter to twelve.'

'That's no time! Why?'

'We're going to a sandy beach further along. There are shops too.'

'We only just got here! I thought you liked this beach because it's away from it all.'

'We can have lunch there.'

'I'd rather stay. I'll make my own lunch.'

'No.'

'Why not? *Dad?*'

'This is a family holiday, sweetheart,' he said. 'The idea is to do things together.'

The idea is to do whatever Gilly wants, I thought, but I didn't say so in case she got stroppy and stopped me going climbing at all. Before I left, I took my mum's photo out of the drawer. I stood it on the chest, turned away from the sun. Let them see who I'd brought on their family holiday.

Downstairs, Gilly was wiping the kitchen table. I swept past without speaking. Arthur ran after me.

'Bye!' he called from the doorway.

I stuck a finger in my mouth and popped my cheek at him. It's been a jokey sign between us since he was little.

I heard Simon's mum playing from outside their cottage, but when Kate let me in, the sound knocked me for six. The cottage looked in shock too with towels,

24

shoes, clothes, plates, music, and books prostrate all over the place.

Kate mouthed an exaggerated hello. She dragged down her cap to cover her eyes.

Sheet music was propped on the mantelpiece, but Kate's mum was long past looking at notes. Her body and the violin dipped and rose as one being. They gave me a bow in rhythm and raced on mad with joy. I'd never seen anything so exciting. I stood there transfixed.

A long note cut off fast. The air went on ringing while it caught its breath.

'This is Leslie,' Kate said.

'Great to meet you! I'm Helen.' Bubbly and laughing, she strode over and pumped my hand. Energy charged out of her. The violin was tucked against her body. I felt I was meeting them both.

'That was amazing!' I said.

Simon clattered downstairs. He grinned at me. 'Hi. We're going rock climbing now, Mum.'

'Brilliant! See you later!'

She smiled full-on as we turned to go. But before the door closed, she and the violin were off again, flinging out currents of wild swirling music.

'She's fantastic!' I said.

'Fanatic!' said Kate.

'Do you two play?'

'I started Suzuki violin when I was little, but it wasn't me.' She grinned. 'I won't tell your brother. I play the drums. Simon plays the piano. Do you play something?'

'No.' I didn't say I refused violin lessons soon after Gilly married Dad. She was at me again to learn piano two years ago when Arthur started violin, but I wasn't going to be set up for cute little duets.

'Mum's practising for a concert tour. Her orchestra's going for three weeks after we get home,' Simon said.

'Doesn't your dad mind?'

Kate said, 'Our gran and gramps come and stay. We haven't got a dad.'

I was all ears.

'Well, we do,' Simon said.

'He can't be bothered with us,' said Kate.

I was stunned she said it so openly. 'That's rough,' I mumbled.

'It stinks,' she said and tugged her cap.

But, I thought, you could go and find him and ask why he can't be bothered. For a second, I wanted to tell them about my mother, but I never told anyone.

This morning the cove shore looked like a prehistoric landscape. Huge naked pink and grey rocks glistened in the sun. The ebb tide unrolled shining waves. Dashes of pearly light on the sea stretched to pure silver near the horizon. The quiet immensity of it all awed me.

Arthur's castle was a pile of stones.

'The sea won,' said Simon. 'Not surprising with another high tide early this morning.'

'He'll be sad,' I said.

'Let's fix it,' said Kate. 'He won't know.'

We did a quick reassemble. The castle didn't look as

26

good as before, but that made its survival more realistic.

Simon spotted the pole where it had floated down the beach.

'There was big trouble about the flag yesterday,' I said. 'It got forgotten. Dad had to come back.'

'Better not use that one again then,' said Simon, grinning.

We set off jumping from rock to rock, each finding our own route. I teetered along the edge of a pool left among the boulders. One foot slipped. I screamed, throwing out my arms for balance.

Simon landed beside me and held out his hand. My heart did its little skip as I took it. His skin felt warm. After I got steady, he hung on a second longer than he needed to. I hoped it was because he liked me.

Further away from the cove, we had to cling like crabs to get round steep damp corners. Waves sucked and gurgled in the gaps below. Once I heard a sound like the breathing of a deep sleeper. Then we came on this embarrassing noise like a wet fart.

Kate said, 'Excuse me!'

Simon snorted. We cracked up. After that, we were really easy together, climbing near each other and helping in difficult places.

We hauled up onto a whopping great boulder bigger than the cottage. It stuck right out into the sea. Here the water frothed like blue milk as it surged over outcrops. A sudden cloud of spray rose in front of us.

'Wild!' shouted Kate.

I looked along the coast and noticed a smudge of darkness. 'Do you think that's a cave?'

'Hey, might be with all this limestone!' exclaimed Simon. 'Let's check it.'

When we got down the other side, jagged pinnacles blocked the view like the ruins of a real castle. We climbed for ages, up and down rock after rock, finding nothing.

'Perhaps that black place was only a shadow,' I said.

Then we came to a steep drop. The sea streamed part way up a channel. At its head, a dark hole gaped between boulders.

# 5

We searched the rock face for hand and footholds. Broken bits made ledges wide enough to rest an edge of trainer. When I was halfway down, Simon beat me by jumping.

Suddenly, I felt his hands on my waist. My heart went as mad as Helen's music. I slid down close to him.

'Thanks.' I turned around, going all tingly. His sparkly eyes met mine for a second.

Kate grabbed our shoulders and skidded between us. 'No smoochy stuff, you two!'

I giggled. I wished I hadn't. I didn't dare look at Simon again.

We tramped over shifting stones in the dry part of the channel and peered into a rocky tunnel.

'Pretty small,' said Simon. 'Might be just the way the boulders fell down the cliff, not a proper cave.'

'Let's see how far back it goes,' said Kate. She stooped and scrambled in.

'Watch out for holes and loose rubble,' called Simon.

He went in front of me. I loved the idea of exploring with him in half-dark, though we had to stay bent over in single file.

The air turned cold. Groping ahead, I got a handful of squelch. 'Yuck!'

'What?' asked Simon.

'Clump of seaweed, I hope.'

'Stinks of dead fish in here, doesn't it? Perhaps they get smashed on the rocks.'

'Or snuff it from pollution,' said Kate. 'Hey, more light.'

She must have stopped, because I bumped into Simon. We said sorry at the same time, but I didn't mind at all, and I hoped he didn't either.

Kate's voice went echoey. 'Oh, *wow*! Excellent. It opens up.'

We stumbled to our feet in empty, shadowy space. A long roof gap let in dim light. Kate sucked in her breath. Behind her, Simon and I started. We grabbed each other, but it was not romantic.

The cave wasn't empty. Below the light, completely still, stood a huge woman.

My chest tightened. A terrible ache shot through me.

For about two seconds, we froze stark as the woman. Then we dived for the tunnel. We tried to jam in together. A stone rattled off the side.

Simon let me go first. I hurtled through, half on my knees. The others fell out beside me. I sat down hard in the channel.

'Flipping heck!' gasped Simon. 'What was that?'

'Or who?' said Kate. The peak of her cap was knocked to the side.

'It must have been a rock, mustn't it?' said Simon. 'It didn't half look like a person. A ginormous woman.'

'Witched into stone like in Narnia.'

'Or that woman in the Bible turned into a pillar of

30

salt. Weird!' Simon looked at me. 'What did you think?'

'Don't know.' I was shocked by the awful feeling I'd had. It was worse than normal scared. It *hurt*.

'It must have been rock,' said Simon. 'No one's that big!' But none of us volunteered to take another look.

Kate straightened her cap. 'Let's fetch a torch, so we can see properly.'

'We won't have time today. Leslie's got to go.'

'Perhaps we'll get witched!' said Kate. She jerked up her arms, fingers spread. She froze into a spiky statue above me, enjoying herself now we weren't going back in.

I tried to laugh. It came out hoarse. I shivered.

'I'm going to see if I can find that gap where the light came in,' Kate said.

Simon gave her a leg up the jumble of boulders beside the tunnel mouth and then sat down by me. 'Are you cold? You've got goosebumps, and you've gone pale.'

He said it so kindly. I had this stupid feeling that I might cry.

'If we come tomorrow, we should wear sweatshirts,' he said. 'People get hypothermia in caves.'

I wanted to answer, but couldn't trust my voice.

Kate yelled, 'It's really steep. I can't get high enough. There's an easier way to get up and down back here though.'

Simon and I climbed where she pointed. She craned up at the fence. Sagging wire squares stretched between metal posts close to the edge. 'Wonder if we could see anything from the cliff top.'

'Don't think there's a path in this direction,' said Simon. 'It's grown over.'

As we climbed back, the dark shape of the giant woman filled my head like a film negative. I tried to figure out the picture. My stomach knotted. I strongly wanted to go in the cave again, but the thought petrified me.

I got so strung up between both feelings that I even forgot Simon. When we were almost at the beach, he surprised me by saying from close by, 'There's your mum and little brother on the rocks.'

'Gilly isn't my mother!' It came out fierce. Simon looked startled. I must have sounded horrible.

Arthur waved and shouted. 'The waves didn't get my castle! They didn't!'

Kate turned and grinned at me. I beckoned her nearer. 'Don't say anything about the cave,' I whispered to her and Simon. 'Gilly's the biggest fusser ever. She'd stop me going.' Whatever we'd found, I wanted it secret from the boss queen.

'Gotcha,' said Kate.

'Leslie, Leslie!' Arthur shouted. 'See how good I climb!'

He was so excited and pleased to see me, I felt mean about abandoning him. When we were back on the beach, I gave him a whirl round. He loves stuff like that.

Simon went to the edge to skim stones.

Helen came down the cliff with a towel over her shoulders. She pumped Gilly's arm. 'Brilliant to have a family in the other cottage!'

'It's great for Leslie to find young people her age,' gushed Gilly.

Kate put her arms around Helen's neck. 'Mum! You didn't say you were going swimming!' It sounded so intimate, I felt jealous.

'The sun told me it was time for a break,' said Helen, laughing. 'Do you want to swim?' She offered the key. 'You could run up and get your things. And Simon's.'

'Don't go in till I'm back!' Kate tore off.

'We heard you playing,' said Gilly brightly. 'Couldn't *believe* it wasn't a recording. Arthur plays the violin, don't you, Arthur? Might we come and listen sometime?'

Her angling made me sick.

'Got your violin with you, Arthur?' asked Helen.

He nodded. Not that he had any choice about it.

'Maybe we could have a jam,' Helen said.

'That would be fabulous,' said Gilly as if Arthur were some prodigy. No way was Book I Suzuki good enough to play with Helen.

'Do you mean eat jam sandwiches?' asked Arthur, amazed at Gilly's enthusiasm.

'Make music together,' Helen said. 'Kate and Simon are great jammers.'

Gilly gushed more delight and then said we must go before the cafés got crowded. She herded me and Arthur away so fast that I could only shout goodbye to Simon. I hoped he didn't think I cut him.

At the cottage, Gilly called for Dad like it was an emergency. He came from round the back with his mobile.

'Reception's hopeless here,' he said.

'Good. Your head can have a rest from radiation!' Gilly said, reminding me to worry that some people said mobiles could cause brain tumours.

After she stampeded us and all the beach clobber into the car, we had to wait for her to go back in because the lavatory window was left open. She's neurotic about burglars. Then she went in *again* because she'd forgotten to leave her necklace in the scallop shell.

# 6

Gilly cunningly chose a hot potato place for lunch. No chance of Dad ordering chips.

But his brain didn't get a break from radiation blasts. The mobile worked OK here. While we waited for our order, he went to the window and talked to someone in his office. The only satisfaction Gilly had was being able to whip away one of the butter portions that came on his plate.

Afterwards, she found a shop that sold organic fruit and vegetables. The rest of us went into a touristy newsagent's with seaside gear and jokes. Dad bought a paper. Arthur trotted about chuckling at Dracula teeth and fake dog pooh, deciding how to spend his money. I wandered through to a boutique part at the back.

There was this turquoise sweatshirt stitched with tiny blue flowers. I held it against me in front of the mirror, noting how my shape showed. I'd only just got curves this year. I'd been dying for them. My friends, Mena and Alice, had been wearing bras for ages.

The colours of the sweatshirt were perfect for me. I'd look terrific wearing it with Simon. But I didn't have enough money.

I went back and asked Dad. 'Please. I won't ask for anything else this holiday.'

'Better talk to Gilly.'

'Why can't you decide?'

He smiled sheepishly.

I put my arm through his. 'Dad, you'd like to give me a present, wouldn't you?'

'Go on, Daddy!' said Arthur.

He was almost won round when Gilly bustled in.

Arthur held up a fishing net he'd bought. 'See what I got.'

She approved. 'You can find out what lives in the rock pools.'

'Leslie wants to buy something,' said Dad.

'A really pretty sweatshirt,' I said.

'You've just had a new long-sleeved top.'

'That was only ordinary.' I looked at Dad, but he wouldn't meet my eyes. He reached for Gilly's shopping.

'Hmm, show me,' she said.

'We'll take the bags to the car while you ladies debate fashion,' said Dad. 'Meet you there.' The coward beat it with Arthur.

I didn't want to buy the sweatshirt with Gilly, but it was my only chance now. I fetched it for her inspection.

'It does suit you,' she admitted.

'It would be good for the beach.' I felt myself blush.

She laughed. '*Wouldn't* it!' I knew she guessed what I was thinking. She untucked the price tag. 'Ouch!'

'I'll use my pocket money. I can pay for almost half.'

'OK then. Treat time. I'll make up the difference. You take care of it now.'

'Thanks.'

'You're welcome,' she said, all gracious like she'd paid for the whole thing.

In the car park, she told Dad she'd given in because I was 'growing up'. She winked at me as if I'd confided something. Some hope! I *hated* her knowing I liked Simon.

A narrow lane with squashed together little houses and shops ran down to the sea. We passed a shop with a big ice-cream cone sign. 'Can we have an ice-cream, Daddy?' Arthur asked.

'Good idea.' Dad grinned at Gilly. 'Like one?' He knew she wouldn't stop us on holiday.

'No thanks. They'll have the noxious commercial kind here.'

'I'll have vanilla,' I said.

At the counter, Arthur asked for strawberry. 'Please,' added Gilly, hovering behind. She couldn't keep out even though she disapproved.

'Pa-leese,' said Arthur.

The woman serving put the cone in his hand. He licked it. 'I'm eating sugar, pink colour, flavour, stablers—'

'Stabilisers,' said Gilly.

'Stabilisers. What else?'

A boy waiting to be served stared. I moved away.

'Emulsifier,' said Gilly.

When we got outside, Arthur said, 'I wish junk didn't taste so nice.'

37

'Quite agree,' said Dad, bits of choc ice dropping onto his chin.

From the promenade above the sandy beach, the sea looked the same cheerful turquoise as my new sweatshirt. I secretly smiled at it.

The beach was crowded. Gilly led the way and selected a spot. She instructed Dad where to put the wind shield to give privacy.

I got into my swimsuit. Gilly slathered Arthur with sun lotion and held it out for me.

'I'm OK,' I said.

'It makes sense to protect yourself.'

I snatched it. 'Oh, here!' Anything to stop a lecture. But after I'd put some on, I handed it to Dad. I didn't want to worry about him getting skin cancer as well as having a car accident, a brain tumour and a heart attack.

Arthur tugged my hand. 'Try my net.'

As we walked over to the rock pools, I found a shell. It was silky smooth like fragile china. The light shone through. I ran back and saved it in my jeans.

Arthur swept a pool with his net. Shrimps darted for cover. I remembered I didn't like nets. Stirring around didn't bring back the shrimps, so Arthur picked up a stone on the edge. He slapped down the net.

'I've got something! Quick! Hold the bucket!'

He shook out a little brown crab. It hit the bucket bottom on its back. We watched it struggle to turn over. It pawed the side.

'He's trying to get out!' Arthur squealed.

'Wouldn't you? Imagine being yanked out of your home and flung upside down into a plastic prison. Don't poke it!'

Arthur yelped. He bawled so loudly that half the beach turned our way.

'What's the matter?'

'He bit me!'

Gilly was on us in a second, hugging Arthur and examining his hand. She yelled for Dad. Some kids gathered round as he puffed over adjusting the waist on his swimming trunks.

'Are crabs ever poisonous?' Gilly demanded.

'Not that I know of. Only jellyfish.'

'That's what I thought. But look at his finger. It's come up in a welt!'

Arthur howled louder. Gilly cuddled him.

'He was jabbing the poor thing,' I said. 'It probably nipped him with its pincers.'

'You're right,' said Dad. 'Lucky it was a little crab, huh?' He ruffled Arthur's hair.

'Nets are cruel,' I said. 'They break bits off crabs and shrimps and stuff.'

'I wasn't going to do that,' wailed Arthur.

'Bet you would have! Everybody does. The helpless creatures get left drying up in the sun.' I glared at the spectators. Some were clutching buckets.

Arthur sobbed and sucked his finger. 'It hurts!'

'I know, lovie,' cooed Gilly. She frowned at me. 'Couldn't you have stopped him touching it?'

'Oh, it's my fault, is it?' Talk about unfair! 'You look after him then! I don't even want to *be* here, remember?'

I ran down the beach. A woman lying on a towel covered her eyes in case I kicked sand.

I slapped along the water's edge and sat on a sticking-up rock. It was a wonder I didn't hate Arthur, the way Gilly went on. Waves floated out of the big sea and lapped my ankles sympathetically. I felt like crying, the same as outside the cave. The image of the witched woman came into my head.

After a while, I saw Dad ambling towards me, stomach wobbling. He shouldn't have had that ice-cream. He was even getting breasts.

I wanted to tell him about the cave. It wouldn't be so scary if he knew. But he'd tell Gilly for sure. It's pathetic when you can't trust your father.

He dipped a fat toe in the water. 'Warmer today,' he said cheerily.

Why did he always have to pretend? I scowled at him. 'I'm forced to trail around with you like a baby. Then the minute something goes wrong, I get the blame.'

'Gilly didn't mean anything. She gets het up easily. She worries about people.'

'Yeah, well, you'd expect her to fuss about Arthur. He's her kid. He doesn't know how lucky he is to have a mother.' I blurted it straight out, though I knew Dad would be upset.

He blinked. 'Gilly's a good mother to you too.'

'Yeah? That's what you think!'

40

'She is. She's always tried hard. She even held back getting pregnant to give you time to get used to her.'

'You told me. Big sacrifice.'

I remember how angry I was when they said she was having a baby. Dad had betrayed me again like when he married Gilly without asking if I wanted her. He was letting her butt another person in between us. Their special kid.

But Arthur turned out OK, mostly. I was the first person he smiled at. Gilly admitted it. When he sat in his baby chair, I'd pop my cheek with a finger. He'd chuckle, so pleased. And after he could crawl, he hung around me all the time.

Dad put on his earnest look. 'Gilly loves you.'

'You must be joking!'

'You don't give her a chance. You hurt her feelings. The trouble is, you've both got strong wills.'

'I'm the one who gets squashed, not her! What about my feelings?'

He wasn't going to listen to them. He was warming up to a wonderful Gilly speech. No thanks.

'Are you coming swimming?' I said.

'Let's get the others.'

'I'm going now.' I waded into the big sea. Out of the corner of my eye, I saw him plod back up the sand.

# 7

Next morning, I woke with a tight fist under my ribs. I considered accidentally on purpose letting out about the cave, so Gilly would forbid me to go. But I couldn't. The cave was calling me. Its secret was the secret of this place. Why the rocks and sea and huge round of sky had been waiting.

At least I was looking forward to Simon seeing me in my new sweatshirt.

'You're not planning to wear that rock climbing, I hope,' Gilly said at breakfast. Dad had walked up the lane to use the phone box, so there were just her and me and Arthur.

'Why not?'

'It's liable to get ripped. Save it for when you're only going swimming.'

'Nothing will happen to it. Anyway, it's up to me if I want to take the risk.'

'Not when I forked out as well.'

'I had to blow all my pocket money!'

'Mum!' squealed Arthur. 'There's a fly on my toast.'

'*Uhh!*' Gilly threw up her hands. 'Put that piece in the bin.'

Arthur started to pick off the fly. 'It's stuck.'

'Don't touch it!' she shrieked.

'Will it pincher?'

'It's covered in germs! Come and wash!'

Arthur placed the fly on his palm and held it out, chuckling. 'Fooled you! It's plastic.'

'Yuck! Where did you get that?'

'The joke shop yesterday.'

I stomped upstairs. I'd have to change or Gilly would make a scene in front of Simon and Kate and spoil wearing the sweatshirt altogether.

They arrived as I was re-combing my hair. When I came down, Gilly was asking Simon about different sorts of rocks. 'It would be *so* interesting if you could help us make a collection.'

Although I loathed the educational angling, I liked Simon knowing stuff she didn't.

Arthur proudly held out his finger. 'A crab pinchered me yesterday.'

'Pinched you,' corrected Gilly, wiping the honey jar. 'It has pincers.'

Kate inspected the finger. 'Can't see anything.'

'There, there!'

'Oh, this weeny red mark.'

'It was BIG yesterday!'

'Bad luck,' said Simon.

'When your dad gets back, we're going to that little supermarket at the petrol station that sells fresh bread,' Gilly told me.

Arthur wrapped himself around my waist. 'I want to go with *you*! I'm a really good rock climber! You saw.'

'Not now,' I said. 'Promise I'll take you another time.'

43

'Oh-wa!' He ran and bounced on the sofa.

'Don't, lovie,' said Gilly. 'You'll break the springs.'

'Got your swimming things?' asked Simon. 'The early tide might not be far enough out yet to climb. Tides are later every day.'

'Where's my swimsuit?' I asked.

'On the line. I rinsed it,' said Gilly. 'But I'm not happy about swimming unless there are adults on the beach.'

'I'm an excellent swimmer!'

Gilly stopped clearing the table and gave me a sharp look. 'It's not a good idea.'

'That's stupid. There are three of us, and we're not little kids!' I turned to Kate to emphasise she was younger than me. 'Your mum doesn't mind, does she?'

Kate shrugged.

'It's OK,' said Simon. 'It'll be warmer later. I've got a Frisbee in my rucksack if we have to wait.'

'Let's *go*!' I said, exasperated. I headed for the door.

'Be careful if the rocks are wet,' Gilly called. 'They'll be slippery.'

'Talk about unreasonable!' I said when we got clear.

'It's just because she doesn't want anything to happen to you,' said Simon.

I didn't tell him it was because she was a control freak. If I said she didn't really care, he might think there was something wrong with me.

He had their car torch in his rucksack. We had a car torch too. But, of course, Gilly had our car locked up the minute we got out. All I could take was my small bedside torch. I'd rammed it down in my jeans' back pocket.

There was no sun yet. The air felt damp. A shivery breeze touched my shoulders. The colours of the pink and grey rocks looked really deep. The sea frothed against them as if it were in a restless mood.

We fixed Arthur's castle again. Simon produced a strip of bright plaid cloth. 'New flag.'

I was touched that he'd bothered. 'That's really kind of you!'

We couldn't get into playing Frisbee. The breeze kept skewing it. After diving for a low catch, Simon sat down on the shingle. He spun the Frisbee on a finger. I guessed he and Kate were nervous about the cave too.

Kate juggled some pebbles.

'Skill!' I said, copying her word.

'You should see her with drumsticks,' said Simon. 'It's a blur.'

When we started along the rocks, we had to jump places where the sea still sloshed around. It was a bit hairy. We giggled when we passed the wet fart, but sobered up on the lookout boulder when we saw the dark hole in the distant cliff side.

'Simon almost told Mum about the cave, but I stopped him in case she told your parents,' Kate said.

'Thanks.' I tried to catch Simon's eye to show I didn't blame him, but he was moving on through the craggy rocks, concentrating on avoiding barnacles.

We got down the easier way into the channel. Simon

45

didn't help me, but I was too churned up by that time to mind. He got out their big torch.

Kate tugged her cap. 'Right, witched woman. We've come visiting. Who's going first?'

I surprised myself by saying, 'I will.'

'Swap torches then.' She handed theirs over.

At first, the torch was reassuring. It lit up ordinary-looking flesh coloured rocks one side of the tunnel and grey-green crumbly layers on the other. But when we got near the cave, it seemed wrong to send the sharp beam ahead. The witched woman might be angry. I clicked off and blinked into the half-dark.

Kate tapped the back of my leg. 'What happened?' she whispered.

Simon also said, 'What?'

I stumbled upright, straining to see. My chest tightened. She was waiting. Her presence was so strong.

'What's wrong with the torch?' hissed Kate, standing up beside me.

I gave it to her and took mine.

She switched on. 'It's OK.'

Like a dare, she shot the light straight at the woman. It spot-lit a giant head with a jagged profile of nose and chin. Beneath the chest ledge, set in cold stone, a cloak fell to the cave floor.

No one spoke. Shivers ran over my back. I hugged myself.

Kate whistled. It rang, echoey, through the cave hollow. '*Some* spell! Dead spooky!'

'The sea does strange things,' said Simon. 'Probably took thousands and thousands of years to wear like that.'

Kate shone the torch at the floor. Slipping on slimy rubble, she started across. I wanted to go with her, but couldn't make my legs work.

The woman was twice as tall as Kate and hugely bigger round. Kate reached out, then jerked back. She wheeled and charged towards us. The light leaped all over the place. 'She's coming alive! Look out! Here she comes!'

A shadow moved behind her. My stomach heaved. I screamed.

'Stop it!' shouted Simon.

Kate tripped and fell. 'Ow!' She rubbed her knee, laughing. 'Couldn't resist.'

He laughed too. 'Dope!'

But the woman *had* moved. Didn't they see? She prevented Kate from touching her. Only I was allowed to do that.

'Can you beat it?' Kate said. 'There's even rubbish in here.' She picked up a plastic bottle. She got up and stood it on a rock over the tunnel.

'Let's check for other passages,' said Simon. 'Go round the sides.'

'Have my torch,' I said, holding it out.

'Thanks.' Our hands touched. The glow lit up his smile.

He picked his way over to the woman and studied the gap in the roof. 'Can't see out. Too narrow.' He went on round to the back of the cave.

Kate spot-lit the stone profile from the other side, dazzling me. 'Yeah, it's best from there,' she called as if I were staying fixed to get a good view. She went after Simon, swinging the beam around the walls. 'See the tidemark where the sea comes in.'

Their voices seemed to dart away with the torches, leaving me and the woman alone in grey air. The light seeping in above was vague, misty. Part of some eerie unfamiliar dimension.

I willed myself forwards. My feet felt heavy and numb. The slippery floor threatened to turn my ankles and send me sprawling. I felt I would fall in a worse way than Kate. I would crack open.

It was so far to get to her. So cold as I got close.

Do it. You're allowed. Slowly, slowly, my fingers opened and spread. My palms homed on the icy body. The terrible ache woke up, in me and *in her*. My mother. My mother was in there!

My mind jolted. Why did I think that? I yanked my hands off. I squeezed them together. They were clammy.

I heard Simon say, 'Looks like the back was hollowed out by the sea and the front is more fallen down cliff. See how the rocks are all anyhow by the entrance and up there where the light comes in.'

'There's earth here,' said Kate. 'Doesn't lead anywhere.'

'Pity.'

The lights dazzled me again as they turned back.

'Want to go? It's freezing,' Kate said. 'Coming, Leslie?'

'Umm.' I pretended to follow them, but fumbled in my pocket for the beautiful shell I'd found on the sand. I was trembling. When the torches were shining on the tunnel, I placed the shell at the bottom of the woman's cloak. A marker. A gift.

A promise that I'd be back.

# 8

Helen was with the others at the cove ready to swim. Arthur raced to me. 'New flag, new flag!'

'Simon brought it,' I said.

He grinned at Simon. 'I *like* it! Thanks!'

He ducked behind me and jumped for a piggyback. I hiked him up.

'You're strong!' said Simon. He ran alongside as I jogged down the beach.

'I've been giving him rides since he was a baby.'

When we stopped, Arthur climbed onto my shoulders. He grabbed my hands. I knew he wanted to show off by flipping over my head and somersaulting to the ground. It was difficult to support him now he was getting heavier, but we managed it.

'And you're an acrobat!' Simon said. Arthur chuckled gleefully.

Kate skipped past and did a handstand on the gritty sand.

'Teach me!' Arthur demanded. 'I'm an aggro-bat.'

Kate lifted his legs. 'This is how aggro-bats hang upside down in caves,' she said. 'They have to watch they don't get witched into stone.'

My stomach clenched. I saw the rock woman waiting in the twilight. I wished Kate realised she wasn't a joke.

Kate let Arthur down and sprang into another

handstand herself. Her cap flopped over her pony tail. Arthur snatched it and scampered up the beach. She was up and after him in a flash. Simon and I ran too.

Arthur dodged behind the rock by the blanket, giggling like mad. I love it when he gets the really hysterical giggles. They shake his whole body like when he used to get the baby chuckles.

Kate dived. They rolled about, squealing, until Kate grabbed her cap. She sat up and pulled it down firmly like a protective helmet, flipping her pony tail through the back.

'Why do you always wear that?' said Arthur.

'I just do.'

Gilly handed me a bag with my swimming gear. 'I brought your things.' Folded on top was my new sweatshirt. 'Thought you might appreciate something fresh when you get out.' She winked, all friendly, as if she hadn't stopped me wearing it. Hypocrite.

'Coming to do some laps, Chris?' she asked Dad brightly. There was as much hope as when she tried to get him to work out with her at the gym, but she never gave up.

'You start. Perhaps I'll come in a minute,' said Dad.

'I'll join you,' offered Helen.

Gilly beamed. 'Will you? Wonderful!'

Dad watched them jog towards the sea. 'Look at that go!' He did a few seconds idiotic running on the spot. His blubber wobbled embarrassingly.

'Dad!' I hugged him still. I felt the roll of fat right round on his back.

51

'I'm digging a trench up to my castle,' Arthur announced.

'That castle is miraculous,' said Dad. He sat down and picked up his book.

After we swam, Kate and I helped Arthur make his channel. Simon went on mucking about in the water, throwing his Frisbee and diving to come up under it. He surfaced quite close and came inshore on his hands.

'Why don't you die when you stay under so long?' asked Arthur.

'I breathe first.'

'Isn't it smothery?'

'What's this smothery?' I asked. 'Did the water go over you at the swimming pool?'

Arthur screwed up his face. 'They make us put our heads under. They *keep* making us.'

I remembered when I was little playing with a blanket with some other kids. They rolled me up in it for a laugh. I couldn't breathe. I couldn't move. It was terrible.

'Silly they,' I said.

Simon said, 'If no one's looking, you can blow good bubbles in swimming pools. The water's calmer.' He blubbered his lips.

Arthur chuckled and blubbered arcs of spit into the air.

'Don't teach him that!' yelled Kate.

She and I went to change behind the windbreak. Simon gave me a twinkly grin when I walked over wearing my new sweatshirt. I'm sure he liked me in it.

We sat on the same rock to eat our sandwiches. He had trouble keeping his together. Chunks of tomato and egg poked out. Helen must have been in a rush.

Her sandwich was in a worse way. She was sitting nodding and smiling as Gilly yakked when a load of stuff bombed out. She gave a quick bubbly laugh. Unconcerned, she picked the pieces off the pebbles and ate them. Gilly made a big effort not to notice. She probably expected her to die of typhoid within the hour.

Arthur threw his crusts to a seagull. Excited shrieks filled the sky. A whole flock of wide flapping wings descended, making me think of angels. We all looked for bits to throw.

'Let's climb the other way tomorrow,' said Kate. 'Search for more you-know.'

'More what?' asked Arthur.

'What-nots,' said Kate. 'But we'll have to wait till we come back. We're going to see some friends that run a pottery.'

'Can I look for what-nots?' asked Arthur.

'Sometime,' I said.

'Tomorrow!' said Arthur. He thumped my back.

'Hey, you!' Simon poked him in the tummy. It felt like he was protecting me.

Later on, when we were about to go up, he said, 'If you're interested, you could come the pottery.'

I was interested in doing anything with him! But it would be a perfect opportunity to go to the cave on my own. I had to grab it.

'I think Gilly has plans for first thing,' I said. 'I'll see you on the beach later.'

He said, 'OK.' He looked at his feet. I was afraid he thought it was a brush-off.

# 9

That evening Gilly announced Dad and I were on supper duty. She laid out salad, pasta and a jar of sauce and reminded us to wash our hands.

'We'll do your violin, shall we?' she asked Arthur, all enthusiastic. She always made out practising was fun. She even learned to play some of the tunes herself on his tiny violin.

'Can you do it upstairs?' I groaned.

Gilly took her necklace out of the scallop shell. 'We planned to,' she said as she fastened it on and smoothed down her hair. 'By the way, you missed your turn washing-up after breakfast.'

'Who says it was my turn?'

'You haven't done any washing-up since we've been here. You haven't helped with anything.'

'Haven't helped! I'm always lugging things from the car or the beach.'

'A lot of it relates to you.'

'We don't need half the stuff. You load us down like donkeys.'

She put a hand on her hip. 'You didn't carry *anything* this morning. You'd have soon complained if we hadn't brought your lunch and swimming things.'

'You wouldn't *let* me take my swimsuit, remember?'

'I only said I didn't want you to go in until we got

55

down there.' She probably wanted credit for bringing my new sweatshirt, but if she'd let me wear it in the first place, there would have been no need.

'Watch this!' yelled Arthur. He tried a handstand against the sofa. 'I'm an aggro-bat.'

'There's certainly one aggro-bat round here,' said Gilly. She marched upstairs.

I stuck out my tongue at her back.

'Leslie,' Dad said quietly.

'Leslie what?'

Arthur's handstand collapsed. He rolled across the floor into the driftwood and lay spread-eagled as if he were dead.

'Up you go, Arthur,' said Dad. 'Mummy's waiting.' He put water on to boil.

Arthur trotted off. When the rasping started, Dad took a Mars bar out of his pocket and ripped it open. Gilly would have had a fit if she saw him – one, for eating a Mars bar and, two, for eating before supper.

'Want some?' he asked.

I broke off a piece. As soon as it was in my mouth, I worried it might give me a spot that Simon would see.

'You eat too much junk,' I said.

'I know,' said Dad like he didn't know at all. He took a big bite.

'You do. You've got breasts!'

'I'm a mammal.'

'You're a male mammal.'

56

'I'm a cuddly male mammal.' He chomped the rest of the bar while I laid the table. He stuffed the wrapper in his pocket and cleared his throat. 'I'm surprised you brought the photo of your mother here.'

Ah! So they had noticed. Probably Gilly nosing to see if I made my bed. I hoped it got her.

'Have you been thinking about her?' Dad asked.

'I'm allowed to think, aren't I?'

'I understand now you're older you wonder about her more.'

Was he an idiot? He couldn't believe that. I've wondered about my mother almost every day I can remember.

He took the lid off the saucepan. Steam misted his face as he tipped in the pasta. 'You reminded me of her when you fussed about the crabs and shrimps yesterday. Sarah caught spiders and wasps in dusters and put them outside. Even got ants and woodlice to walk on paper so she could carry them out.'

I liked hearing that. Gilly couldn't kill wasps fast enough. She absolutely freaked out once when some flying ants came in the kitchen.

'Did I ever tell you about the day I took that photo?' said Dad.

'You never talk about my mum at all!'

'Well . . . it's difficult.'

'Because Gilly wants to pretend you and Mum were never married, doesn't she?'

'Of course not,' he mumbled. He stirred the pasta. I

was afraid he'd shut up. I sat down at the table with my chin on my fist, perfectly still.

He said, 'The day of the photo, Sarah and I were celebrating. We'd just found out she was expecting you. You can see how happy she was.'

The sweet smile. For me. Why then?

'The idea of us making a family meant so much to her,' said Dad. 'Her parents divorced when she was a toddler. Your grandmother started her business. Sarah spent most of her time with childminders.'

I knew my Australian gran was a workaholic. Twice she had written she was coming to see me. Then some work project stopped her.

'Mum felt unwanted?' I said.

'And I believe your grandmother had a temper.'

'You mean she hit her?'

'I don't know. It must have been difficult for her on her own. I know Sarah did her best to get rid of the childminders.'

'Gilly's hit me.' Only a couple of times and not for ages, but the thought of it still made me fume. 'She never hits Arthur!'

Dad was silent. I wished we hadn't got back on to Gilly. I was desperate for him to talk about Mum. He should have told me more stuff like this before.

'So if she was happy about making a family, what happened?' I asked.

'I don't think it's something you can pin down to one cause. Your grandmother talks about post-natal depression. Hormones can get mixed up after having a baby. But Sarah was seeing a psychiatrist in Australia before she went backpacking. She told me, but I didn't realise how truly bad she felt about herself.'

He stared into the saucepan. The steam condensed on his face like sweat. 'We had about six good months and then ... Sometimes I'd come home and she'd be lying on the sofa in the dark.'

'Didn't she have a job?'

'Yes, but I worked later. I was trying to do well for both our sakes. She said she was proud of me. She'd go over the top about how much cleverer than her I was. It wasn't true. She was always running herself down ... '

He clamped on the saucepan lid. 'I just wanted you to know about that picture.' He buttered a piece of bread.

'But if she *really* wanted a baby—'

'She was ill. When the pain got strong, she didn't tune in to good things.' He folded the bread the way Gilly hates and started stuffing it.

I needed to sort this. I searched for the right questions.

Dad rooted in a cupboard. 'Here's a pan we can use for the sauce,' he mumbled with his mouth full. 'You could put that salad in a bowl.' He wanted me to leave it now. He'd made a big effort. Done his duty. Couldn't handle anymore. *Pathetic*. But I didn't ask anything else, because I felt sorry for him.

As soon as I'd fixed the salad, I ran upstairs and studied the photo. *I was in it.* I was a secret only the three of us knew – my parents and little me, growing inside my mum. For sure, it was still secret. Dad wouldn't have told Gilly that.

In bed later, I kept thinking about the spiders and wasps and especially Mum leaning against the tree, happy she was going to have me. It didn't make sense. As I tossed about, the tree turned into the witched figure in the cave. It closed around the happy Mum, filling me with dread.

# 10

Simon's family's car was gone in the morning when we walked by to the beach. It made me feel empty. Part of me screamed I was an idiot not to go with them. I listened for the sound of the sea to reassure me I was doing the right thing.

Going down the path, I saw a bright flutter near the water. 'My flag's flying!' shouted Arthur. He started to run.

Gilly grabbed him. 'Not so fast!'

'Let go, Mummy!' He wriggled free.

'Then walk sensibly.'

The castle stood smartly upright, pole in the middle. Simon and Kate must have fixed it before they left. Magnum nice! I prayed I hadn't put Simon off me.

It was frustrating waiting for the tide to get far enough out to climb. I was also anxious about getting away from Arthur. Luckily, a family with little kids arrived. Gilly sucked up to the parents, and pretty soon he was playing with the tinies.

Dad avoided laps by swimming with me. Gilly's Amazon training meant she did more each day. She was still at it after we were out and dressed.

I moved towards the rocks, pretending to search for interesting pebbles. When Arthur's back was turned, I scrambled over the boulders on the edge of the beach and carried on fast.

The dark hole looked even scarier on my own. I clicked on my torch and crept in. The damp fishy stink hit me. I kept the torch beam on the ground to avoid the squelchy seaweed. Rotting fish might be tangled up with it.

I crouched where the tunnel emptied into the cave, my little light becoming hardly more than a candle. A hurting longing gnawed inside me.

'Mum? Are you there?' I whispered. 'It's Leslie. Can I come in?'

The cave was dead still. Far away, muffled waves broke again and again. My body rocked as I waited. This was my mother's place. She lived in the stony shadows. All the years, she had been waiting for me to find her.

My eyes adjusted to the gloom. The jagged face became clear. I stared at it, begging for a sign. 'You wanted me to come, didn't you?'

Only the breaking waves answered.

I trod carefully across and shone the torch on the bottom of her cloak. The special shell was gone! Dismayed, I held the torch closer. The sea must have moved the shell. Why hadn't I put it up high where her chest made a ledge?

But it seemed like she'd been careless too. 'Why didn't you look after my present, Mum? It was so pretty!'

I clawed through pebbles and grit to show her, to give it to her again. It *mustn't* be lost! I searched the floor all the way to the tunnel and back, desperately overturning stones and poking through slime. But it wasn't there. The ache in me grew worse.

I leaned against her body. I thought of Kate snuggling up to Helen. 'Mum, help me! I feel so awful!'

My eyes prickled. 'Why did you leave me to horrible Gilly? She only took me on because she wanted Dad. She'd rather it was just Dad and her and Arthur.'

I shoved the torch into my pocket, so I could hug her. She was rigid and cold. My fingers stroked a smooth place. How long would it take for stroking to wear away rock and let out what was inside? Let out my mum, mum, mum. I'd never been able to call anyone Mum. It wasn't *fair*.

Tears ran down my cheeks. I wanted to feel her arms around me like they must have been once. Did the nurse lift me up onto her after I was born, skin against skin? Was she happy that her baby had arrived safely? Was I the most important thing in the whole world?

I longed to be the most important thing in the world to her now. 'You *wanted* me! Why didn't you stay?'

It was very dark inside my head. The stone hurt my forehead, but I pressed into it harder. In the darkness behind my eyelids, I saw a small girl crying.

The girl's mother was in a hurry. She pushed her away with a fake smile. When the girl clung on, the mother got angry. She prised her off. A door clicked shut. The girl knew that where her mother was going was more important than she was.

I wanted to cuddle her. I wanted to say, 'You're lovely. You're precious. Your mummy's lost out by leaving you.'

I knew the little girl wasn't me. This was happening a long time ago in Australia, and that tiny girl was my mother.

I leaned there for a long time, crying.

# 11

Near the cove, I climbed close to the cliff and kept low. Dad was lying on the blanket reading, head propped on a towel folded over a stone. Arthur was chasing around with the other little kids while Gilly jabbered to their parents. I made sure she was looking the other way and jumped down.

I headed for Dad. I wanted to tell him that I'd found Mum. That she'd shown me what it was like when she was a little girl. That it made me feel terrible. That I didn't ever want to see my Australian gran. I hated her.

Gilly spotted me and hurried over. She held Arthur's trunks and armbands. She'd probably tried to coax him into swimming when the other kids did.

'Where have you been?' she demanded.

'Just climbing around.'

'Don't disappear like that! You've been ages.' She scrutinised my face. 'You're not getting a cold, are you?'

'No!' The crying must show. Why couldn't she leave me alone?

'If you feel one coming on, take vitamin C. I brought some.'

'I'm not getting a cold!'

'OK. Don't bite my head off.' Martyr voice.

She sat down by Dad and started rattling on about a garden the other people had visited. There wasn't a chance of talking to him. And it suddenly seemed hopeless that he would understand. He'd probably think I was going bonkers. He'd discuss it with Gilly. They'd send *me* to a psychiatrist.

The family were leaving. I wandered down to the water where Arthur was trailing his net along the edge. Gilly still carried the nasty thing around with the beach clobber to emphasise her disregard of my opinion about its cruelty.

'You went rock climbing without me again,' Arthur accused.

'You were playing.'

'I'd rather have gone with you. You promised we'd go.'

I glanced at the path down the cliff. If I weren't here when Simon came, he'd really think I was avoiding him, but probably there was a bit of time.

'Want to go now?'

'*Yea*-eh!' He raced to Dad and Gilly, shouting, 'Rock, rock, rock! Me and Leslie are going rock climbing.'

'OK, if you're careful,' said Gilly. 'Look after him, won't you, Les.'

'*Leslie!* I wouldn't say I'd take him if I weren't going to!'

'At least the tide's well out. Shall we have lunch first?'

'No. We won't be long.'

'Yes, long!' Arthur insisted.

'Look at the time,' Gilly said. She reached for the bags. 'Let's eat first. You must be hungry.'

'I'm not.'

Dad clapped his book shut, ready to act the creep. 'I'm certainly feeling peckish.'

I glared at Gilly. 'I thought you *asked*. *Shall we have lunch now* and I said *No*.'

'Majority rules,' said Dad.

'You must be joking.'

'Try being a bit appreciative!' Gilly snapped. 'You don't offer to help *make* the lunch.'

Boss, blame, boss, blame. This was what I got for being nice to Arthur. Now I was trapped. I ate fast, but Arthur didn't. I told him to bring the banana he wanted after his sandwich.

'It won't be safe to climb with something in his hand,' said Gilly.

I folded my arms and stared while he finished the banana, his drink and then took a biscuit.

'Arthur!' I howled.

'Oh, I won't have it.'

'Don't be silly,' said Gilly. 'For heaven's sake, relax, Leslie! We're on holiday.'

Arthur handed the biscuit to Dad and started in the direction of the cave.

'Let's go the other way,' I said.

'You like this way,' he said. 'It must be good.'

'But I've never been the other side. Help me explore it.'

'We'll go this way next time, huh?'

'Maybe,' I said noncommittally.

We were on the first rocks, when Gilly called, 'You-hoo!'

More delay! 'Don't look,' I said to Arthur through clenched teeth. 'Unless you come now, we're not going!'

'Don't you like them anymore?' asked Arthur.

I turned and saw Kate and Simon on the path. We'd almost missed them! 'OK, let's wait.'

But although it was obvious we were waiting, they stopped by the blanket. Gilly smiled and gabbled. She gestured in our direction. I was embarrassed in case she was telling them to come with us, and Simon didn't want to.

They ran over, Simon a bit behind Kate.

'We're rock climbing,' said Arthur. 'You can look for what-nots if you want, but you have to come now because Leslie's in a hurry.'

Kate laughed, but it sounded like I'd tried to get away without them.

'I didn't know when you'd be back,' I said, feeling myself blush. 'Do you mind going slow for Arthur?'

'You don't need to go slow!' said Arthur. He jumped to another rock.

Actually, he turned out to be a good climber for a little kid. I hardly had to help him. Simon didn't climb near us or say much. I was afraid I'd blown it.

We found a big shallow rock pool with a sandy bottom. 'I won't catch anything,' Arthur said to me. 'I wouldn't even if I had my net.'

'Good.'

'Feel how warm it is,' said Kate. She took off her trainers to paddle. It was sunny, and we were all wearing shorts.

Simon sat on the edge. I felt awkward, so I got ready to paddle too.

'Is this a what-not?' asked Arthur.

'It's calm water,' said Simon. He bent down and blubbed bubbles.

Arthur did his air blubber spray. Kate blew an imitation of the wet fart at him.

'You're gross!' said Simon. 'Splash her, Arthur.'

Arthur chuckled. He flicked an arc with the back of his hand. Kate jumped in and ran to the middle. She sent a shower back. Simon suddenly splashed me. He grinned. Things were OK between us! I plunged after Kate.

'Let's get them!' said Simon.

'Yeah!' Arthur pulled off his trainers.

Simon held out his hand. They slopped in and chased us, kicking water. We chucked it back. Arthur loved it. He doubled over with the hysterical giggles.

Then he let go of Simon to splash with both hands. He lurched and lost his balance. He fell backwards. The back of his head hit the water. His shorts and T-shirt went under.

His face screwed up with fright. I rushed towards him, waiting for the howl.

But Simon grabbed him under the armpits. 'Whoops!' he said. He towed him towards the side. Before they got there, Arthur was laughing.

'Again!' he squealed. I couldn't believe it.

Simon towed him around the pool. Kate gave me a secret thumbs up.

'You're swimming on your back!' I said. Arthur chuckled and kicked his legs.

Returning to the beach, I whispered to Simon, 'You were brilliant! You should be giving him swimming lessons.' His eyes went twinkly.

Arthur galloped across the shingle to Dad and Gilly, shouting, 'I fell in! I fell in!' I ran after him.

Gilly leaped up, staring at his clinging clothes. 'Are you all right?' she shrieked. She scanned his body for injuries. 'What happened?'

Why did she have to make a scene? No wonder the kid developed phobias. 'Splashing game,' I said.

'Tell me what happened! Did he fall off the rocks? How far was it? Why weren't you watching him?'

'It was only in a rock pool *in a splashing game*!' I said. 'Geez, you never listen.'

Gilly noticed Simon and Kate hanging back. She clapped a hand on her chest and smiled at them as if I'd wound her up. 'Oh! You frightened me! As long as nobody was hurt.'

'You can see he's not hurt!'

She peeled off Arthur's top. 'Chris, hand me his sweatshirt and swimming trunks.'

'I'm not swimming,' said Arthur as definite as ever, his excitement gone. She'd wrecked all the benefit of him having fun in the water.

'You need dry things on, or you'll catch cold,' Gilly said.

Her eyes darted to check if my suspected cold was developing. The feeling of wanting to cry clutched my chest again. I glowered at her to stop it taking hold.

'We've got a treat now,' she said, rubbing Arthur with a towel. 'Did Kate and Simon tell you? Helen's asked us for a jam.'

'Are you jamming, Simon?' Arthur asked.

'You betcha.'

'Then I am.' He allowed Gilly to help him into his trunks.

'How can you?' I asked Simon. 'There's no piano.'

'You could come and see.' He looked down like he was afraid of another excuse.

I didn't hesitate. 'Thanks, I will.'

# 12

We trooped up the cliff. Dad said he had to put some time in on a report. He was really sorry to miss the jam. Faker.

Gilly fetched Arthur's violin. She hurried through the open doorway of Simon's cottage and gaped. Then she faked too, pretending not to notice the chaos.

'Brilliant!' bubbled Helen when Arthur got out his pint-sized violin. They conferred over tuning. I hoped the poor kid wasn't going to be shown up because of Gilly's stupid manoeuvring.

Simon cleared chairs for her and me. He placed them on the edge of the kitchen area. 'This is so exciting!' Gilly gushed.

Kate came downstairs tossing a hand drum. 'Pity I haven't got my whole kit. I whack a wicked cymbal.'

Simon shoved aside the clobber on the kitchen table and put down an electric keyboard. He grinned at me. 'My portable keys.' I grinned back.

Kate perched on the end of the bench. She wedged her drum between her knees and gave her cap a tug. 'O-*K*!' She beat a roll. 'Take it away, group!'

They started with Arthur's first Suzuki piece. Although I thought I'd never voluntarily listen to *Twinkle, Twinkle Little Star*, I got a kick out of seeing Arthur standing all proud, playing with the others. I hadn't ever really wanted to put him off playing. It was Gilly's manipulation that got me. I also thought how appropriate the piece was for Simon's sparkly eyes.

They played the livened-up Suzuki variations. Helen tapped her feet. Gilly started clapping along. She can't keep out of anything.

Helen and Simon looked at Kate. The beat changed to an even jazzier one. Arthur chuckled. He bowed in and hit most of the notes.

'Way to go!' called Simon.

They played another of Arthur's tunes. Helen kept with Arthur while Simon played a harmony. It was a real turn-on to see how good he was. Then Simon played with Arthur and Helen's fingers danced over the strings, swirling ribbons of extra notes around the melody.

With just a glance, they tossed the lead to each other. It made me wish I could play something. It seemed hardly any time before Helen called, 'Fantastic! Thanks, everybody!' Her bubbly laugh circled the music-makers.

'Skill!' confirmed Kate, giving her drum a final rap.

'Oh!' cried Gilly, pouting disappointment.

But Helen knew to stop before Arthur had enough. 'Who'd like to christen our new mugs?' she asked. 'Our potter friends made them. They're gorgeous.'

They were. They had slate blue glazes. The colour of another of the sea's moods.

The others went outside with their drinks, but Simon showed me some cool sound effects on the keyboard.

'Want to go and explore the cliff path?' he asked.

'Great.' I didn't know if he was asking me on my own, but I wasn't going to muff it.

Kate and Arthur were playing swing ball behind the cottage. Gilly and Helen sat in deck chairs under a tree. Gilly was blabbing non-stop like Helen was getting her whole life story. We just walked away down the track.

At the cliff top, the direction of the cave was overgrown and fenced off. A path on the other side started through gorse, but quickly opened out to run along the edge at the bottom of a field.

There was so much space on the cliff – up, down, behind and in the vast round of air over the shiny sea. You felt yourself expand into the space, like you could just float off. It was terrific being up there with Simon.

Though it had seemed quite far when we were climbing along the beach, we were soon over the rock pool. Simon said, 'I think this path goes all the way to that headland and down into the next village.'

'Let's go to the headland!' I said.

'You want to walk that far?'

I wanted to walk with him forever! I nodded.

'What time is it?'

I looked at my watch. 'Twenty to five.'

'It'll take at least three-quarters of an hour. Maybe more. Is that OK?'

''Course.' Gilly was a stickler for meal times, but they weren't the same on holiday. I couldn't be expected to know what she planned today.

A flock of gulls rose from the shore. As they passed,

I heard their easy angel wing flaps. They gathered high above us, curved and headed out over the water. They dwindled to specks and melted into the endless sky.

'You wonder how they know to all turn at the same instant,' I said.

'There're other ways of knowing than words.' Simon tapped my arm with his finger as if making a point. He ran the finger down my bare skin. I didn't move. I think I stopped breathing. He drew a circle or perhaps a question mark on the back of my hand. Then his other fingers tucked in. We were holding hands!

I was idiotically happy. I wondered if he held hands with girls all the time. I hoped not.

Our hands stayed warm together until the path went narrow between brambles and we had to let go. But there was a steep bit where we looked over. We were really close. I wondered if he'd kiss me. I wanted him to, but he didn't. Perhaps it was too soon to kiss someone after you'd just started holding hands.

An older girl and boy with backpacks strode up.

'Hi,' said Simon as we let them past.

'Hi yuh,' said the girl, without reducing speed.

'Somewhere they want to get tonight,' said Simon.

My mother left Australia backpacking. Where did she want to get to? A place where people showed they loved her. She'd found Dad. Dad loved her. But Dad works a lot like my Australian gran. Did Mum mind? Why didn't she say if she didn't like it? Why didn't he guess? It hurt so much that they hadn't made things right.

'What's up?' said Simon.

'Nothing.'

'You were frowning. Want to go back?'

'No, no.' I wanted to be here with him. I was wasting it!

# 13

We held hands wherever the path was wide enough. The wind lifted Simon's hair and made red bits glint in the sun. There was the lovely fresh smell of sea. Everything was wonderful, excellent, supreme!

But the headland was farther than it looked. I glanced at my watch when we got there. Five to six. I didn't say anything. Stuff Gilly. This was more important.

We walked to the point. An old couple sat on a bench, looking out to the horizon.

Simon dropped onto long grass. 'We made it!' He plucked a stem and lay back in the sunlight, chewing the end.

I leaned on an elbow beside him. My heart ka-plunked while I wondered if I had the nerve to touch him. Why not? He'd started the holding hands.

I stroked the hair off his forehead. Just one stroke. He closed his eyes and sighed, 'Ah!' The hand holding the grass slid to the ground.

I risked another stroke. He smiled, eyes staying closed. I glanced to see if the old couple disapproved. They were still gazing at the sea. The man had his arm tucked through the woman's. Her hand rested on his leg. They looked peaceful.

We were quiet too.

Simon said, 'Suppose we should go.' He didn't move. 'I don't want to.'

'Me neither,' he said. He must like me!

If I had the nerve, it would be really easy to lean over and kiss him. But I wanted him to kiss me. Otherwise I couldn't be *sure* he liked me that way.

He sat up. I sat up beside him. His face turned towards me. Then he jumped. This huge wet dog ran at us, wagging its tail. No sign of an owner. It must have come up the path from the village.

The dog seemed to think we were its owners. It nuzzled in, trying to get on our laps. We scrambled up. Although I was cross with it, I had to laugh, the way it crouched and cocked its head ready to play.

'No sticks up here, boy,' said Simon, patting him. 'It's not safe. Dogs sometimes fall off cliffs and get killed.'

I grunted at the grisly thought. I looked at the sea tumbling over rocks far below.

'The tide's coming in,' said Simon. 'What time is it?'

'About six thirty.'

'Already! We better go.'

The dog followed us. 'Go home,' I said. 'You'll get lost.'

The old couple called it, trying to be helpful. It trotted to them. They smiled and waved. I liked seeing how companionable they were. They seemed to enjoy being together as much as I liked being with Simon.

We held hands again where there was room, but Simon walked faster than before. I slowed down and looked over when we were almost back.

'Rock pool's gone.' I hoped there might still be the chance of a kiss.

Simon said, 'Yeah,' but didn't stop. 'Will you be in trouble for being away so long?'

'I'm always being got at for something.'

'Are you?' he said.

That panicked me in case he thought I did awful things. 'Will you be in trouble?' I asked.

'Mum's a bit vague about times, but I usually tell her if I'm going to be gone long. Want me to call to her and then come back with you?'

'It's OK.'

I was glad he didn't. When I opened the door, Gilly sprang up from sweeping under the kitchen table. Dad spun round from the sofa. Arthur stared from the floor where he'd made a driftwood car route.

Gilly put her hands on her hips, scowling. 'Just where do you think you've been?'

'For a walk.'

'We waited and *waited* to have supper! It was practically ruined!'

'I didn't want you to wait. How can I be expected to know what you plan? It's not that late.'

'You know perfectly well we eat before this! Why didn't you say where you were going? We were worried. I hope getting into boys isn't going to make you even more inconsiderate. I *assume* you were with Simon, since he was missing too.'

I cringed. She'd probably made a scene with Helen.

Simon would hear about it. I'd look a right baby.

'Why do you have to know where I am every minute?' I demanded.

Arthur sent a car whizzing across the room. It overturned.

'You're lucky you've got responsible parents!' snapped Gilly.

'A warder, you mean!'

Dad leaped in to defend her. 'That's no way to talk. Apologise.'

'I apologise for going more than two metres without an electronic tag.'

Gilly glared. 'You drive my patience to the limit!'

'That's something we've got in common then,' I said.

'You are *so rude*! After I let you buy that expensive top too. You're never grateful for anything! Perhaps you should stop her pocket money until she learns a better attitude, Chris.'

'You can't do that! I'm skint.'

'We're not having cheek,' said Dad. 'Another word and you *will* lose pocket money.'

Gilly was itching to egg him on, so I gave her a dagger look and clammed up.

She put my supper on the table, martyr silent. All the pans and plates were left stacked in the sink. I knew why, and I wasn't going to let her have the satisfaction of giving the order. The minute I'd finished, I washed up the lot.

# 14

Next morning, Gilly opened the door to Simon and Kate all hypocritical hospitable.

'Hello, there! Come on in.' Not a whisper about the walk. If she blamed Simon, she might mess up Arthur's chances of more musical inspiration or educational rock identification.

When her back was turned, I smiled at him. He smiled back with his magic twinkly look. My heart ka-thumped.

'Everyone's invited to a picnic on the beach at five o'clock,' said Kate.

'How kind!' gushed Gilly. 'That will fit with our day nicely. What shall I bring?'

''S OK. We're going shopping after Mum's finished practising. Want to help collect driftwood ready for the fire, Leslie?'

'Can I, can I?' piped Arthur.

'You betcha,' said Simon.

'That'll be all right for an hour,' Gilly said. 'Then we need to leave.' She was dragging us off to the garden the people on the beach told her about. Right in the middle of the day when the tide would be out. The best time to visit Mum.

'Do I *have* to go?' I said, hoping she would relent in front of Simon and Kate.

'Yes.' She gave me her sharp look, then switched back to pretend friendly. 'We'll be back well before five. Now *no* falling in rock pools today!'

On the way to the beach, Kate said, 'Your dad came looking for you yesterday evening.'

'Gilly probably sent him.'

'I told him not to worry. You and Simon would be off smooching somewhere.'

'You didn't really, did you!' I said aghast.

Kate laughed.

'Smoochy-coochy!' sang Arthur. 'Leslie and Simon are smoochy-coochy!'

My face went hot. Simon poked Arthur and said, 'Hey, you!' I didn't know if that meant he minded or not.

'Your mum didn't say anything?' I asked quickly.

'She was playing the violin most of the time,' said Kate.

'Can't compete with the love of her life!' said Simon. 'No, I'm kidding. She cares as much as your parents. She's just a different sort of person.'

Different from Gilly all right. He had no idea what I put up with.

At the bottom of the cliff, he tapped his head. 'Uh-oh!'

He and Kate and I looked at each other. We'd all forgotten the castle.

Arthur ran to the edge and gaped at water running back from a tumble of stones. The flag pole lay between them. Grit covered the sodden flag.

'They got it! It's all-fall-down!' he cried. He grabbed the pole and smacked the water. 'Stupid waves!'

'All-fall-down is why there are rocks to climb,' said Simon. 'The sea knocks them off the cliff. Humungous all-fall-downs!'

'Why didn't the castle get knocked down the other days?' Arthur demanded.

'We played a trick on you,' I said. 'We fixed it before you saw.'

I wished we hadn't when I saw how he minded. His lips trembled as he struggled to take it as a joke.

Kate tugged her cap. 'We'll make it again.' She started rebuilding.

'No, let's get wood.' Arthur headed up the beach, dragging the pole.

Simon followed him. 'See, after the rocks crash, they get broken into sand. Then sand and stuff gets buried and squashed and makes rocks again.'

Arthur nodded and made a fist. 'Sandrock.'

'Sandstone. You remembered!' Simon said. 'And the limestone rocks are made from broken shells. Things are always changing.' He smiled at Arthur.

Arthur studied him. He smiled back and started walking faster. I felt warm watching them.

We piled up sticks, a salty plank, and a broken crate that we found half-buried under the cliff. It was stamped with words in an alphabet we didn't recognise.

Kate hauled a hunk of tree stump from a crevice above the beach. It must have been thrown during a storm. She sent it bumping down to whack the shingle. Pebbles flew like spray.

'Have to save the biggies till last,' she said, sliding down after it. 'We can't have a roarer while we're cooking. Mum's going to buy some charcoal.'

I made sure Arthur and I weren't longer than an hour. I *had* to go to the cave today. We must get back from Gilly's trip with enough time before the picnic.

She caused another delay leaving. Not about the necklace. She left that in the shell most of the time now. But when Dad backed onto the lane, she noticed towels on the line. She insisted on taking them inside in case someone nicked them while we were out.

'Honestly!' I said when she got out of the car.

'Come on, sweetheart. Make an effort,' pleaded Dad as if I were the reason everything between us wasn't hunky-dory.

I might have liked the garden if it hadn't stopped me going to Mum, and if Gilly hadn't been there. She sauntered along holding Dad's hand and reading labels with stories about the plants. The stories were interesting, but it was really irritating the way she read loudly so Arthur and I would be sure to hear.

She tried to hoodwink me into getting involved. 'This one about deadly nightshade is faded. Can you make it out?' she asked innocently. I told her I couldn't.

I went ahead and sat on a bench. When they caught up, I said I was hungry. We were having lunch in the garden café.

'Yesterday you weren't hungry. Today you want lunch early,' Dad commented cheerily.

'She wants to smoochy-coochy with Simon,' said Arthur.

'Stop being silly!' I snapped.

Gilly grinned at Dad. He laughed like they'd been talking about me and Simon. I hated it.

After lunch, Gilly went into the shop. She pounced on a book about pebbles. 'Oh, let's buy this.' She gave me a teasing look. 'We'll show Simon.'

'He knows what they are already,' I said and walked off.

I saw a postcard rack. It would be cool to write to Mena and Alice about Simon. I also remembered Mena had brought me a present from her holiday.

There were some cute little notepads with leaping dolphins decorating the edge. They weren't expensive. I took two postcards and two dolphin notepads to where Gilly waited in the queue.

'Can you get these for Mena and Alice?'

'You are not having any more money this week,' she said, stiffening.

'But I'm broke! They're for my friends!'

'You should have thought of them before you spent everything on yourself.'

'Please!'

'I'll buy the postcards, but that's all. It won't hurt you to think about the consequences of your behaviour for once.'

Talk about mean. She wouldn't even *lend* me the money. And, of course, once she'd said no, Dad couldn't either.

At the cottage, I couldn't get away fast enough. When Gilly went in the lavatory, I darted out and legged it down the lane.

I hoped no one was looking out of the windows at Simon's. I tore down the track, wondering what I'd do if they were already on the beach. At the top of the cliff, I scanned the cove, but there were only two women swimming.

Seeing Mum felt really urgent. I ran past the driftwood pile and clambered over the rocks. Now I knew the best route, it didn't take as long.

I'd forgotten my torch, but I didn't care. I ducked straight into the tunnel and groped along, not worrying whether I touched seaweed. Bursting into the cave's dim light, I went slipping across and fell against Mum.

'I'm here!' I hugged her. I kissed her too. Part of me wondered if I *were* crazy, but another part felt such relief to be with her.

I slid down and sat on the bottom of the cloak on a place that wasn't too damp. I tried to picture her smiling sweetly like in my photo.

'Are you feeling better today, Mum? I'm really sorry about when you were little, but *we* love each other, don't we? That's what's important.' I waited a minute, hoping she would find a way to confirm she loved me, but she was concentrating on listening.

'Yeah, I can talk to you, can't I?' I said. 'I can trust you. You're my *mum*!' What did I want to tell her, my own true, loving mum?

'You know that boy that came in here before? I'm pretty sure he likes me, and he's really nice! It's amazing. I feel so happy when I'm with him, I forget about living with horrible Gilly.'

I paused and stroked her, wishing the stone weren't cold. 'You must have felt great when you found Dad, and he loved you. You loved him too, didn't you? You look like you do in my photo.'

That photo was a real day, bright and hopeful, with me growing inside her. 'Whatever happened with stinking Gran, you had him and you had me. You could have got him not to work so much. We were on the way to making a good family. Why did you stop believing in us?'

I began to feel choked up. Gran wrote about post-natal depression. An awful thought shot into my head. 'Did you stop loving me after I was born? Did I disappoint you?'

Perhaps I cried too much. She probably wanted a chuckly baby like Arthur. Maybe I seemed crabby. Maybe I wore her out. Maybe she wished she'd never had me.

'I can't help the way I am! Some people are just naturally nice like Simon, and some people are horrid cows like Gilly. I'm not that bad anyway. OK, I fight with Gilly, but I wouldn't have with you. Tell me you love me. Do you, Mum?'

I pressed my face against her. And there it was again. Terrible blackness. It pressed from every direction. It swallowed me. No safety anywhere. No right to be safe.

'Oh, Mum! Don't feel like that! Was it my fault? Don't let it be my fault. Tell me what to do to make it better.'

My brain fogged up. I could hardly think. I pulled back from the rock. My energy was zapped like my blood had turned to water.

'Mum, you *were* witched,' I whispered. 'Those bad feelings witched you, and they're witching me.'

I had to get out in the sun.

I staggered to the tunnel and crawled along. I leaned against a boulder by the entrance, breathing heavily. The channel seemed to sway. Put your head between your legs, I told myself. Geez, this was awful. I mustn't come here anymore.

But I wanted her! *I wanted my mum to love me*.

# 15

When I got to the lane, Gilly and Arthur were turning into the garden of the other cottage. Gilly had changed her clothes. She looked like a stupid sailing ad model in a striped T-shirt and tight white pants.

'Leslie, Leslie!' called Arthur.

'I thought you were helping get the picnic ready,' said Gilly. 'Where are the others?'

'I don't know.'

'Where have you been?'

'Nowhere.'

'What kind of answer is that?' She scrutinised me. 'Are you feeling all right?'

'Of course!'

She frowned and shook her head. 'Go and fetch the bag with the swimming things from by the door. I've got the blanket and the windbreak. I'll see if there's anything we can do. Oh!' Her hand leaped to her mouth. 'Don't know if I shut the lavatory window. Tell Dad to check it's locked before he comes.'

'Why do you open it if you're going to be so neurotic?'

'So it won't get smelly.'

'Smelly belly,' sang Arthur. 'Don't get a smelly belly, Leslie.'

I ignored him. 'I'm going.'

'Don't get a smelly belly and go,' Arthur shouted, giggling. He wanted me to laugh too, but I wasn't in the mood for infantile jokes.

Dad was sitting on the sofa, typing into his laptop with one hand and eating a Mars bar with the other. He must have had a stash of them somewhere. Shows how completely useless it is to tell people not to do what they want to.

'OK, sweetheart?' he asked absentmindedly.

I moved his papers onto the shelf by the shell containing Gilly's necklace. I sat beside him. 'Dad, did I cry a lot when I was a baby?'

His face tensed. I could tell he wished I wouldn't bring up the past again, but he answered cheerily, 'All babies cry. Life's rain and sun.' He offered to break off a piece of Mars bar.

'No thanks. Did I cry *a lot*?'

'You were a normal healthy baby.'

'Are you sure there was nothing wrong with me?'

'Not a thing.' He pretended to study the computer screen, but I wasn't letting him off.

'Is post-natal depression always to do with hormones?'

'That's one theory.' He sighed and finally looked at me. 'I told you, your mum was ill before she got pregnant.'

'But was I the last straw? Was I, Dad? I want to know.'

'You were the best straw. Cross my heart. She wanted you so much. She went on and on about how she wasn't going to be like her mother.'

90

'After I was born she went on about it?'

'Yes!'

'So what stopped her? Didn't she think you loved her anymore?'

His face crumbled like he might cry. My stomach lurched.

'Oh, Leslie, I hope – I believe – she knew I loved her. I did, I did!' His hands clenched the laptop for a second, as if he were trying to make it give evidence. Then they went limp and flabby.

'The trouble was, when she felt bad, she thought she wasn't worth anything. I think she got this idea she wasn't good enough for us, you or me, that we'd be better off without her.'

'That's stupid! Why didn't you make her see it wasn't true?'

'I tried. As much as I understood. But I didn't realise what was going on in her head. I didn't ever think – I didn't know how much help she needed. I've been over and over it. So many things I wish I'd done differently.'

He looked at me helplessly. He put his arm around my shoulders, but it seemed like it was mostly to get comfort himself. It made me angry. I didn't want to have to feel sorry for him. I wanted him to feel sorry for me!

He wasn't going to. I had to get away from his pain. I shrugged off his arm and stood up. 'Her majesty commanded me to tell you to shut the lavatory window when you come.'

'Don't talk like that!'

I started for the stairs. He called after me. 'We're lucky to have Gilly!' It sounded like he was scared of losing her too.

I sat on my bed, feeling shaky. No sound came from downstairs.

After a while, I put on my new sweatshirt. My hand trembled as I combed my hair. In a minute, I'd be with Simon and that was great. I'd go to the picnic and muck about and like it, but it wouldn't be all of me.

Perhaps it had been the same for Mum. Perhaps she hid her blackest feelings.

# 16

The swimming bag was the usual monster weight. Gilly had even jammed her new pebble identification tome down the side. I lugged the bag to the other cottage and dropped it outside the open doorway.

Kate was collecting cutlery from plates on the sitting room floor for Simon to wash. Gilly was cutting rolls in half.

'Hello, hello!' Helen called gaily. 'Almost ready!' She stuck a finger in the dressing she'd made and licked it. Gilly struggled to hide her horror.

Helen wiped her hand on her jeans. 'Now where did I put that bag of marshmallows?'

Ha! I stole another look at Gilly's face. Neat sugar!

Helen went to look in the car. Kate shoved drink cans into a backpack. 'Yum,' said Arthur. 'We get Coke. Coke rots your guts.'

Kate laughed. 'I thought it was your teeth.'

'I'm afraid it's not good for the rest of you either,' said Gilly, unable to control herself any longer.

'Spare us the sermon,' I groaned. Immediately, I felt cross. She'd made me sound grumpy in front of Simon.

He didn't understand what a trial she was, not even when she constantly butted in on the beach. As soon as we got down there she tried to boss everything.

'We don't want to leave ashes scattered where people

93

sit,' she said, looking about to decide the place for the fire.

'We found a sheltered spot over at the side,' Simon said patiently as if he agreed.

He and Kate and I had a quick swim and then got ready to cook. They'd brought a special big frying pan from home to balance on stones. We scraped a hole for the charcoal in the middle.

After she finished her million laps, Gilly was back with girl guide advice about letting the flames die down to make a hot bed under the pan.

I glared at her. 'That's what we're doing!'

'OK, OK,' she said, sounding like she was always pacifying my bad temper. Then she went on about being careful the oil didn't spit while we were cooking the veggie-sausages.

Dad arrived. He did his isn't-this-jolly routine. No hint of our conversation.

There was loads of food. Helen laid it out on a worn plaid tablecloth with a familiar pattern. One corner was ragged.

I looked at Simon. 'The flag?'

He laughed.

'Didn't your mum mind?'

'Nah, it was torn anyway. It's ancient.'

'Gilly would flip if I ripped a bit off something she still used!'

He just laughed again.

While we were eating, Gilly tried surreptitiously to

move away anything she disapproved of that landed near Dad, Arthur or me. I made a point of getting up and moving back anything I wanted.

We got sticks from the woodpile to toast the fat pink and white marshmallows. Arthur grabbed his flagpole. 'On here! On here!'

He wrapped the flag around to make a handle. Gilly insisted on wiping the other end before he speared a marshmallow. 'Be careful, or you'll burn yourself.' She hovered behind, ready to rescue him from imminent incineration. Every time someone's marshmallow caught fire, she squealed, 'Watch out!' I don't know how the others stuck it.

She tried to organise us into playing Frisbee. She tossed the Frisbee to Dad.

'I'm too full!' he moaned.

'How about starting our rock collection then?'

Kate juggled some pebbles. Arthur chuckled with delight.

'Want to make a pebble shy?' Kate asked him.

'Yeah, yeah!'

They lined up a pyramid of empty drink cans on a boulder. Rows of five, two and one.

'Roll up!' shouted Kate. 'Three pebbles. Contestants stand three times their height away.'

Arthur lay down and turned over. 'I'm rolling up!'

'OK, you first. One point for each knock-over.'

Gilly moved to watch.

Arthur hit the boulder twice, then got the hang of

aiming higher and sent the top can flying. We clapped.

Helen jumped up, scooping stones. She threw two of them with fast overarms. They missed. She grazed a can with a careful underarm, but it only rocked.

'Close,' said Gilly.

Helen laughed. 'I'd better stick to fiddling!'

'Arthur leads,' announced Kate. He clapped himself.

Dad trundled over, all good-sporty. 'Look at this! Three strikes.'

He tossed, mouth open, and got two cans. The next stone missed. The last toppled two more. 'Harder than it looks.'

'Four!' Kate called, re-setting the shy.

Arthur tugged Gilly. 'You, Mummy.'

'In a minute.'

Kate used skimming technique, but only flipped off one can. I went for bigger stones. They were a bit heavy. My first fell short, but I got the can in the bottom middle with the next. It crashed with the three above.

'Shot!' called Simon.

But now the end cans were stranded. I chose the ones on the left. The stone whizzed past.

'You're tied with your dad,' said Kate.

'Here comes the tie-breaker,' said Simon. He walked to the side.

'What are you doing over there?' demanded Kate.

'Yeah, Simon, you should stand on the tied line!' shouted Arthur.

'I'm three times my height away. You didn't say anything about angle.'

'Go on then,' Kate agreed.

Simon's first pebble took off the end can. I saw his idea. He was trying to knock the bottom row cans into each other. Then none would be left stranded. The ones above would fall automatically.

He threw harder and toppled the next can in line with two above. His third strike got two more.

'Six!' called Kate. 'Skill! Simon in the lead. Last contestant!'

Gilly took her time selecting pebbles, smaller than mine, but bigger than Kate's. She swung her arm to warm up like it was the Olympics. I bet she loved the idea of whacking those Coke logos. She went to throw from where Simon had stood.

'You're not three times your height away,' I said.

'Just having a look first,' she said, giving me an exaggerated smile and moving back.

Jaw set, she aimed with a fierce underarm. Smash! Cans rolled every which way. Four over. She strode to the other side of the stack and threw again. Smash! Only one left. She stepped back to aim from the centre. And wouldn't you know? She cleared the deck.

Everyone except me clapped and cheered. She bowed!

'Sneak!' I said. 'You went last so you could plan your strategy from what we did!'

'I'd say that was pretty clever,' said Dad.

Gilly pouted, mocking me. 'Weren't we allowed tactics?'

My face went hot. Now she'd made me look a poor loser.

'Again! Again!' yelled Arthur, setting up the cans. I had to join in, but I felt so angry, I didn't hit anything in the next round.

# 17

The sun left the cove. I was longing for it to get dark, but this time of year night came late and morning early.

Helen packed up and went to practise. Dad helped her carry the picnic gear on his way back to his laptop.

'See you in a little while,' Helen called to Gilly.

Kate and Simon lifted the tree stump and swung it onto the fire.

'Mind the sparks!' Gilly yelled. She held Arthur. He struggled loose. He got his flag stick and copied Kate poking at the stump through the flames. Gilly watched, sharp-eyed. Soon she said it was time for them to go up.

'Not yet!' he protested.

'Daddy's got a new book for you tonight.' She had him. He loved the novelty of Dad reading to him.

'I expect you three want to stay a bit longer,' Gilly said as if she were granting a big favour. 'I've filled this bottle for you to put water on the fire before you leave.'

'Nothing's going to catch alight down here,' I said.

'Best to be safe,' she said in her know-all voice. She rolled up the windbreak. She also took the bag with the swimming things. Probably to make sure we didn't go in again.

'Why's she seeing your mum later?' I asked Kate.

'Mum's giving her a lesson.'

'Giving *her* a lesson?'

'Didn't you know she's always wanted to play the violin? Her parents wouldn't pay for her to learn.'

'Don't tell me I'm going to have two of them scraping away!'

Simon laughed.

'Bad luck if she goes as mad as Mum,' said Kate. 'Hey, let's see how high we can get the fire.'

We combed the beach for every scrap of wood left. We chucked it all on at once. The flames flared, snapping and crackling like live things. Smoke billowed up and away out of the cove.

Kate shuffled through the pebbles. 'Bah, ba-bah!' She started to jive.

Simon clicked his fingers and swayed.

They were so into it that I only hesitated a second before joining in. Soon the three of us were bopping around, belting out songs from the charts over the roar of the fire. I wished Arthur could have been there. He'd have loved it.

When the blaze died back, we flopped on the blanket, giggling. Dusk had finally come. Rosy firelight flickered on the rocks and on Simon and Kate.

'I've never had a fire on the beach before,' I said. 'It's so neat. Your big frying pan was perfect for cooking.'

'Yeah, we've had it since Dad went on holiday with us,' said Simon.

Kate grunted. 'Years ago!'

'Three years,' said Simon.

'Don't you ever see him?'

'He's moved away,' Kate said. 'He lives with this woman miles younger. You know what gets me? *His* father left. He knows what it feels like.'

'He blocks it out,' said Simon.

Kate grunted again and pulled her cap over her eyes.

'Mum says Dad can't face phoning or writing because he feels bad about hurting us,' said Simon.

'So he hurts us more by pretending we don't exist!'

I looked at Simon. He didn't seem angry like Kate. 'Don't you mind?' I asked.

'Of course. I'd tons rather he'd stayed. But this is how it is. Everybody has something that gets them. There's a boy in my class has to go round in a wheelchair.'

'That's bad. But it's bad losing your dad or mum too.' Lots of terrible things happened to people, but that didn't stop your own awful things hurting.

He nodded. 'How old were you when your mum went?'

'Three months.' I swallowed. It felt like I had a piece of rock in my throat. 'She killed herself.'

'Oh, *Les*lie!' said Kate. And on my other side, Simon moved nearer and took my hand. They didn't make me feel ashamed. It felt good that I'd been able to say what happened.

Stars began to show. The beach tucked itself around the glowing embers. Waves broke and shushed peacefully.

'Tide's started to go out,' said Simon. 'Be low in the middle of the night and back in full just before we come down tomorrow.'

After a bit, Kate gathered her stuff and said, 'Think I'll go up.'

Simon and I watched her shadow disappear against the cliff. We didn't move. Our arms and legs touched in the warm firelight. I felt close to him inside too. A piece of wood fell deeper into the embers. I felt sure he would kiss me.

Then someone crunched towards us. Kate was back. 'Your step-mum's up there,' she said. 'She wants you to come in too.'

I could have growled. I was so embarrassed and *so* angry!

Simon poured Gilly's water on the fire and shoved the bottle in his rucksack. Kate helped me fold the blanket. The three of us climbed the path. Gilly stood at the top, hands resting casually on the hips of her tight white trousers.

I held in my fury as we went up the track. 'You're welcome to come back with us for a while,' Gilly chirped to Simon.

He glanced at me, but I kept quiet. I could just imagine the horror of sitting around with everyone smirking. And it would be even more embarrassing to go and perch on the bed in my tiny freezing room, even supposing Gilly let us.

Simon said, 'No thanks. Think I'll go in too.'

We said goodnight awkwardly. Maybe he was back to thinking I didn't want to be with him. And I did! It had been *perfect* on the beach. Gilly was wrecking the best thing that ever happened to me!

I stomped up the lane. 'Why did you have to come and fetch me?' I demanded when we were out of earshot.

'I don't want you wandering off late at night. There are hazards around coasts in the dark.'

'We were right where you left us!'

'I couldn't have much confidence you'd stay put after yesterday.'

'STOP TREATING ME LIKE A TWO-YEAR-OLD!'

'I am *not*!' Gilly snapped. 'Your dad agreed you should come in.'

As if Dad ever dared disagree. 'You just enjoy ruining things!'

'Watch how you speak to me! You've been warned!'

If I didn't shut up, she'd have the satisfaction of getting my pocket money stopped. Geez, I hated her!

I thought of the cave. I longed to go and tell Mum how unfair it all was, but the memory of the witched feelings was too scary.

# 18

In the morning, Gilly announced we were driving further down the coast. She fixed me with a severe look. 'No complaints! You can see Simon and Kate when we get back. And we'll stay around here tomorrow, since it's our last full day.'

'Why can't we stay today? Arthur likes it here. You like mucking about with Kate and Simon, don't you, Arthur?'

She didn't let him answer. 'We're going to *try* and have a nice family day out. We get little enough time to do things together.'

I glanced at Dad. He went on breezily washing up breakfast bowls. No chance of any support.

As we were loading the car, Simon came up the lane. He grinned like he was looking for me. Perhaps he hadn't been put off by last night! Heart thumping, I ran out of the garden. I told him I was being dragged off again.

'Ask if you can have supper with us,' he said. 'Come as soon as you're back. You can stay all evening.'

'Terrific!' Helen wouldn't mind if we went off by ourselves. I'd make sure it was somewhere where Gilly couldn't interrupt.

Simon came to the car with me. Gilly was all graciousness. *Of course* it would be fine for me to go for a meal. How kind of them to ask.

'See you later,' he said. Eyes sparkling, he gave everyone a wave.

Gilly got out the map and directed Dad which roads to take. It was easy to ignore her. I leaned back, daydreaming about a walk in the dark with Simon.

We arrived at a sandy beach. It wasn't as crowded as the other one. Gilly was delighted with her *find* until we discovered oil all over the place. Then she nagged constantly about watching where we put things.

In the afternoon, we passed an estuary and drove inland. She gave an irritating lecture on river water emptying into the sea, being sucked up into clouds and raining inland to make rivers again. After about ten minutes, Dad turned into a car park.

'Why are we stopping?' I asked.

'Going on the river,' said Dad with fake enthusiasm.

'Oh, no! I thought we were going back now.'

'Don't be a misery-guts. This will be fun!' said Gilly.

We trudged over to a shack with an open counter on one side. Dad asked if this was where to hire the boats. The man nodded and pointed to a price list on the wall. Dad asked for a rowing boat.

'Can't we have a motor boat?' I said.

'Certainly not!' exclaimed Gilly. 'Rowing is a wonderful sport.' She winked at the man. He went on dealing with Dad's credit card.

'Have you got life jackets?' Gilly asked. 'We'll need a small one for my little boy.'

The man rummaged under the counter and hauled

some up. Gilly made a big fuss about getting them on properly, but I didn't let her fiddle with mine.

After the man collected two oars, we followed him to one of the boats tied to wooden decking beside the river.

'Step into the centre,' Gilly instructed. 'Arthur, there's a special little seat for you behind the bow.' She pointed to the front of the boat. Trust her to know the right word.

'Leslie, you sit in the stern with Dad.' Boss, boss, boss.

When Dad got in, the boat really rocked. He lost his balance and sat down hard. The boat lurched.

Arthur squealed. 'Are we going to sink?'

'No, it's only the ballast moving about,' said Gilly, taking the middle seat.

'What's ba-last?'

Gilly grinned at Dad. 'Heavy weight.'

'You know you like me cuddly,' said Dad.

The man squatted beside us and fitted the oars in the rowlocks. Gilly helped needlessly. When he undid the rope, she leaned back and pulled through the water with know-all efficiency. We glided into the middle of the river.

'Do you think that chap can talk?' said Dad. 'He didn't say one word the whole time.'

'The silent type,' said Gilly.

Dad laughed like she'd said something funny.

I ploughed the water with my hand as we turned downriver. Gilly smugly whooshed past a boat rowed by a woman in a red T-shirt. The woman looked miffed.

The oars dipped and rose. Gilly's face came towards us with each dip. I noticed she was getting lines around her eyes. She would hate that! Something she couldn't control.

'You're a good rower, Mummy,' said Arthur.

'I worked at a water sports centre one summer when I was seventeen.'

Wouldn't you guess? Organising people right back then.

'You might like to do something like that one day, Leslie,' she said.

Not if you did, I thought.

'Can you go faster?' asked Arthur.

She picked up the rhythm and really started moving it. Muscles bulged in her arms.

She kept it up for ages before getting breathless. 'There! Someone else have a turn. Leslie?'

I shook my head.

'Let's see what Dad can do then. Come on, Chris.'

She held the oars as Dad obediently switched seats. The boat rocked. Waves slapped the sides.

'Ba-last, ba-last,' said Arthur.

Dad plunged the oars. 'Heave. Ho!' We shot forward, not smoothly, but definitely fast.

Arthur chuckled. 'Good, Daddy!'

'Oh, *knots* quicker than me!' said Gilly.

Dad laughed and pulled harder. He was showing off.

'Maybe we should turn around though,' Gilly said. 'It'll take longer going against the current.'

Dad single oared. We swung near the bank and just got round.

107

He dug into the water, trying to get back to a fast pace. But it took much more effort now. His neck went pink. Veins bulged in his forehead. Sweat soaked his shirt underarms. I got worried.

I waited for Gilly to tell him to ease up. Perhaps she hadn't noticed he was overdoing it. I glanced at her out of the corner of an eye. She sat beside me, watching him and grinning. What was the matter with her? He could have a heart attack out here! He could be dead before we got to the landing.

Finally, I couldn't stand it. 'Oh, I'll have go!'

'Marvellous!' gasped Dad.

I ducked forward. He went on his knees to get to my seat. He was panting like a dog.

Gilly laughed. 'Believe me now about needing to get fit?'

I could have kicked her. She'd set him up. I swung the oars back smartly. They smacked the water. Dad wiped the splash over his face. 'Blessed cool!'

'Edge of the blade down,' Gilly said.

It put me right off. I rowed through the air.

Arthur giggled.

'Keep the oars close to the side of the boat,' instructed Gilly. 'Straighten your back.'

I realised too late that I was set up too – a sitting duck for her criticism. Angrily, I concentrated on dipping the right amount and not splashing, but somehow I pulled harder on one side.

'Are we turning round again?' asked Arthur.

'More left oar,' said Gilly. 'Bring your hands up to your chest.'

I rested the oars and glared at her. 'I can't do it, if you keep on at me!'

'I'm only trying to help.'

'Yeah, expert at everything. Bet you got the water sports medal first time you took a boat out.'

'Now, now,' puffed Dad. 'Come on, we're drifting back.'

I sat rigid. 'I'm not rowing till she stops carping.'

Gilly stiffened. She tightened her lips. 'It's very immature not to be able to take advice.'

We glared at each other.

Arthur slid about on his seat. 'Ba-last mo-ving! Ba-last mo-ving!'

'Come on, Leslie,' pleaded Dad.

Gilly turned her head sharply. 'We're going to hit the bank!' she shrieked. 'Out of the way!'

She lunged at me. I jumped to get clear. My knee struck one of the oars. The handle thrust up between us as the boat jolted into mud. The oar flipped into the water.

'Now look what you've done!' Gilly yelled.

'You knocked me!'

'Get it quick!'

I leaned over. The oar floated out of reach.

Dad made a grab, but missed too. The boat tipped sideways, almost taking in water. Arthur screamed.

'For heaven's sake! Keep still!' ordered Gilly. 'I'll push out to it.'

She yanked the other oar free and rammed the bank. The boat swayed, but remained stuck. The escaped oar drifted towards the middle of the river.

'Chris! Push from the back!' demanded Gilly, changing orders. Dad stretched over the other side and groped through a tangle of weeds.

'Hurry!' yelled Gilly. 'If we don't catch it soon, it'll be off to the sea!'

Great. And I'd be getting flak for the next year for something that was her fault. I pulled off my sandals. Before they noticed, I was up on the seat and over the side.

# 19

The boat lurched behind me as I hit the water.

'No, Leslie!' cried Dad.

'What do you think you're *doing*?' screeched Gilly. 'Get back in here!'

The life jacket rose and bumped my neck. I felt furious with Gilly for making me wear it. The oar bobbed into the current and sped away. I swam really hard. I touched the end, but it stayed ahead.

Dad yelled, '*Come back!*' He sounded angry and scared. What if he leapt in after me? The shock of cold water after overheating could give him a heart attack.

I kicked like mad and made another grab at the oar. This time I got hold, but it had turned into a slippery pole that didn't want anymore to do with boats.

It wouldn't tuck under my arm. When I tugged, it wrestled and skewed, pulling me downriver. The bank swept by.

'LEAVE IT!' bellowed Dad. 'NOW!'

Treading water, I glanced back. Dad and Gilly had stopped trying to free the boat. They were both shouting. Gilly beckoned with dramatic scoops of the air. I was shocked at how far away they looked. I wasn't going to be able to tug the oar all that distance against the current. I had to let go.

The oar floated gaily away. I was so frustrated! Now

I'd be in big trouble for jumping in for nothing.

I turned to swim upstream. It was really difficult. I struggled, but my energy got used up staying in the same place. A fist of water shot up from under the life jacket. It went into my mouth, making me gag.

'*Swim across the current!*' screamed Gilly. Of course! Why hadn't I remembered that?

I headed diagonally out of the middle of river. It was immediately easier. Near the bank, my feet touched the muddy bottom. I cleared my throat and spat. I half walked and half swam to the boat.

'In at the back, or you'll tip us!' Gilly yelled.

'You naughty girl!' cried Dad, helping me. 'Are you all right?'

'Of course I'm all right!' I crawled, dripping, onto the seat. Arthur stared at me with a pinched-up face.

'I can't *believe* you would be so stupid!' shouted Gilly. 'What possessed you? Jumping into a current like that! Thank goodness for the life jacket!'

'It made it harder to swim!'

'You had it on too loose! I told you. At least it kept you afloat.' She threw back her head and sighed. 'Heaven knows what we'll have to pay for that oar!'

'It wasn't my fault it came loose! You jumped at me!'

'Who got in a sulk and made us hit the bank? What a mess! We can't paddle a rowing boat upstream with an oar. I better get out and walk back for help.' She gave the overgrown bank a martyr look. 'You've certainly excelled yourself in ruining a nice day out!'

112

'I'll walk back,' said Dad, and then glanced upriver as we heard a drone. A motor boat ploughed towards us.

'Get them to go after the oar!' I said.

'It's gone!' snapped Gilly.

'A motor boat could catch it.'

Gilly waved wildly. The boat slowed, rocking us with its wash. 'Could you possibly tow us to the landing?' she called. 'A young idiot here has lost one of the oars.'

My face burned. 'It's only just floated away,' I said loudly, hoping they'd take the hint. But Gilly went straight on about tying the rope to the hook on the back of their boat.

She moved Arthur to the middle seat. He clung to it as the boats bumped and wobbled into position. Gilly knelt on the bow, making a big deal of knowing the sort of knot that wouldn't slip.

She gave non-stop advice as the motor boat jerked us around. It tugged us humiliatingly slowly past other boats. The woman in the red T-shirt watched from the wooden decking.

'Bit of trouble?' she said when we got out.

Gilly gave a fake laugh. '*Someone* lost an oar,' she said coyly. She nodded at me struggling to undo my wet life jacket. The tapes were tangled.

'It wasn't my fault!' I protested.

Gilly raised her eyebrows to make me seem a liar. She gushed thanks at the motor boat people. Dad shook hands with them. He piled up our life jackets and went to settle with the silent boat hirer. Arthur trailed after him.

113

Gilly pushed my shoulder. 'You – to the car! Come on, you're shivering.'

She strode ahead and unlocked the car doors. 'Take off your things and wrap up in the towels and jackets,' she ordered.

'No way! I'll put a towel round me, but I'm not taking my clothes off.' I could just see Simon coming over when we pulled up and me not able to get out.

She thrust a hand on her hip impatiently. 'You're asking to catch pneumonia, and you'll expect me to look after you!'

'You're the last person on earth I'd want to look after me!'

She glared. 'You can be really nasty! Move then!' She shoved me aside. She yanked bottles of mineral water out of a plastic bag and arranged them on the back shelf. She slapped down the bag. 'Sit on that or the seat will be wet for days.'

Dad came across the car park holding Arthur's hand. Gilly got in the front and slammed the door. Dad glanced at her anxiously as he settled Arthur into his seat belt. Arthur hunched up, sucking his thumb.

'What did you have to pay for the oar?' Gilly demanded.

'Only the cost of replacement,' Dad muttered.

'How much?'

'The deposit plus five.'

'THIRTY-FIVE POUNDS!' She twisted round and shouted, 'That's your pocket money gone for a good while!' She'd got her stinking way at last!

'*It wasn't my fault!*' I yelled. 'And if we'd asked the people in the motor boat to go after the oar, we wouldn't have had to pay at all!'

'Just be quiet, Leslie,' barked Dad.

'Are you going to let her reduce me to poverty for something that wasn't my fault?'

'*Be quiet!*'

He was totally in her power. I folded my arms and looked daggers at his back. I know he saw in the mirror. When we got to the cottage, he made an excuse about needing to get petrol. He took Arthur with him.

Before we got inside, Gilly laid into me again. 'You realise that besides putting yourself in danger, you terrified your little brother. It's going to be even harder to get him over his fear of going in the water now.'

'It's your fault he's scared in the first place. Forcing him to go to those swimming lessons. The instructors are rubbish.'

'Don't be ridiculous.' She unlocked the door and marched into the kitchen with her bags.

I went after her. 'Arthur doesn't trust them! He let Simon tow him about the rock pool when he fell in, no trouble. He wasn't frightened then. Those instructors make him put his face under.'

'You can't swim if you don't get over worrying about your face getting wet!'

'He's afraid he's going to smother!'

She flushed. 'First I've heard of it.'

115

'He keeps saying he doesn't like going! It's always the same. You ignore what we feel. Whatever you decide is right. It doesn't matter what the rest of us think!'

'You're so ungrateful! I put a *huge* effort into thinking what's best for everybody.'

'Controlling everybody, bossing everybody, you mean!'

'*Looking after* everybody!' she yelled. Her face and neck were blotchy red.

'Yeah? You know why I volunteered to row? Because Dad was completely blown-out. His pulse must have been going a million a minute! He could have had a heart attack out there on the river! You're supposed to be worried about him having a heart attack. But you were *so clever* making him exercise, you didn't see what was happening! You could have *killed* him!'

She flew at me. She whacked the side of my head.

I pressed my hand to my stinging ear. 'You make people deaf doing that! Shows how much you care, doesn't it?'

'You can stay in your room the rest of the day!' she screamed. 'I'm sick of your hurtful insolence!'

The spiteful cow wasn't going to let me go to Simon's!

'And I'm sick of you,' I hissed. 'I wish *you* were dead!'

116

# 20

I was seething. Simon and I had hardly any time left. This would have been the most fantastic night of my life.

When I got out of the shower, Gilly was carrying on to Dad downstairs. You could probably hear the wailing and sobbing from the beach. She tried *so hard*. *Day after day*, she put up with sulks and insults. I treated her like *muck*.

Dad's voice was muffled. He must have been hugging her. He said, 'I know, I know.' Not a single word on my side!

An hour later, he brought a tray up to my cell. He put it on the chest behind Mum's picture and the postcards I didn't feel like writing now everything was spoilt.

'Here's something to eat, though you don't deserve it. You've upset Gilly terribly.'

'Did she tell you she hit me?' I asked.

'You provoke her. You must stop!'

'It's OK for her to beat me up, is it?'

'Don't exaggerate! She feels bad about slapping you. She doesn't believe in hitting children.'

'That's a joke then. She wants to control all of us, and she can't even control herself! I didn't do anything except tell her the truth. It's so unfair! Let me go to Simon's, Dad!'

'No.'

'They're expecting me.'

'Arthur's been to say you can't come.'

'Thanks a lot!'

'Leslie, you've got to change your behaviour.'

'Tell her to change! She's got no right to rule everything I do! My mum would never have treated me like this.'

He looked at me wearily, but I didn't fall for it.

'*She wouldn't have!*' I shouted.

'You don't know what your mother might have done. Concentrate on how you treat people.' He lumbered out, shoulders slouched.

He might feel bad about Mum, but he'd completely switched loyalty to Gilly. Well, I hadn't switched! I'd go and see Mum again, because, however scary it was, I belonged to her not Gilly.

I undid the window catch, but the arm was locked to open only a few centimetres. No chance of getting out that way. It didn't matter, because it gave me an idea. During the rest of the horrible evening, I had one pleasure – plotting my revenge.

I left the curtains back so I wouldn't oversleep. Grey light filled the window when I woke. It was just gone five thirty. Low tide was in the middle of the night, probably only a couple of hours ago. I could still easily get along the rocks.

I put on my new sweatshirt. I was finished with Gilly dictating every minutia of my life. But I wore my waterproof on top, because I noticed the hedge blowing outside. I tiptoed to the stairs.

Arthur's door was ajar. The bunk bed creaked as he turned over. I waited a second for him to settle, then crept down and quietly opened the lavatory window. I laid the spare lavatory roll on the floor like it had been kicked over.

In the kitchen, I jabbed a straw into one of the small orange juice cartons and drank it. I grabbed an apple and a bag with some dates left from yesterday's picnic. I shoved them into my pocket with the main thing.

Gilly insisted the key stay hooked next to the door in case of fire, so it was easy to let myself out. The wind covered the slight noise I made lifting a dustbin under the lavatory window. Then I was off down the lane.

The curtains were closed in Simon's cottage. I pictured him sleeping. That felt nice. I'd be back to meet him as soon as he got up. I wasn't letting anything wreck today.

I'd make him understand how last night was all Gilly's fault. We could exchange addresses. Maybe I'd secretly take the train to London, and we could meet. I liked the thought of pulling that one on Gilly.

I ate a date going down to the beach and another as I climbed. The sea was rough. The rocks at the edge were getting hammered. Waves poured off the lookout boulder in waterfalls. A piece of wood was being tossed and battered in the swirling water crashing over the outcrops. The oar was probably somewhere out there this morning, turning into driftwood.

I scrambled on. Gulls called overhead, free-wheeling

119

in the wind. In front of the cave, waves hissed halfway up the channel, flinging shingle and scraping it back.

As I tramped to the entrance, one of the gulls swooped and coasted above. I glanced up into her round eye. She squawked. It went right through me.

'That's what you know!' I said defiantly.

I clicked on my torch and ducked into the tunnel, glad to be away from the tugging wind and the din of the sea.

I stopped when I got into the cave. Mum's human shape became visible through the dim haze. It gave me a fresh shock. I wasn't going loopy. She was here!

'I've brought you something beautiful,' I said. 'You'll want to keep this safe.' Eagerly, I went across and showed her in the light of my little torch.

It did look beautiful as I let it hang below my fingers. It swung slightly. The light gleamed on the delicate swirls like the first time I saw it long ago. My stomach clenched. My chest filled with pain.

'It should be yours. If you'd stayed with us, Dad would have given it to you. If you hadn't been witched by those bad feelings.' I felt terrible. Her bad feelings, my bad feelings, Dad's bad feelings.

'You *were* good enough, Mum. Dad wanted you. I wanted you. I've always wanted you!'

I reached up and carefully put the necklace on her chest ledge. 'Do you like it? I brought it to show I love you. I don't want you to feel bad anymore.' I stroked her as I waited for a sign. I closed my eyes, crying again.

'Come back, Mum. *Please* come back and love me.' I

120

didn't dare lean against her. I couldn't take more of the blackness.

'You don't know the trouble I'll be in if Gilly finds out I took the necklace.' My burglar trail through the lavatory window might not be convincing. And if I didn't make it to my room before they woke up, she'd suspect me for sure.

'She's got Dad ganging up against me now. *Mum!* I need you!'

There was no sign. Mum didn't move. She stood there *unmoved*.

My chest hurt like it was being gouged. 'Don't you care what happens to me?' I sobbed. 'What kind of mother are you?' I kicked her. 'Wake up! Stop shutting me out! You're worse than Gran. You didn't leave me *even one memory*!'

Nothing I could do would make a difference. She shut me out when I was three months old. She left me alone in my cot and emptied a bottle of pills. Even though she could make it right now, she wouldn't.

'Stay dead then! See if I care!' Tears burned down my face. I stumbled over the slimy stones. My inside felt raw.

I crawled out of the tunnel. The sea rushed towards me, crashing higher up the channel.

Someone called, 'Leslie!'

I stared. There, crouched on top of the drop, hair standing up in the wind, was Arthur.

## 21

'What are you doing here?' I gasped.

'I wanted to know where you were going,' Arthur called over the crashing of the waves.

'You followed me all this way!' How could I not have noticed?

'You didn't look round once.' He chuckled.

'Does anyone know you're out?'

He shook his head. 'Is that a cave?'

'It's nothing much.' I blew my nose.

'I want to see inside. Catch me.'

'No way. We're going straight back.'

'I can get down myself.' His trainers scrabbled over the edge. Pyjama bottoms poked from under his jeans.

'Wait!' I ran across.

He slid into my arms. 'Why are you crying? Is it scary in there?'

'Yes. No.' Perhaps scary would sound exciting. 'You shouldn't have followed me! Why can't you mind your own business? We've got to get back. The tide's coming in.'

'We'll be quick. Promise, promise!'

'Gilly will go spare if she wakes up. I'll get the blame, not you!'

'Just one peep. Please!'

It was going to be quicker to let him. 'You're a

*nuisance*! All right, but you're to come straight back and tiptoe upstairs like we haven't been out, OK?'

'OK.'

I went first and shone the torch behind me at the floor of the tunnel so he could avoid touching the seaweed.

'This is a what-not, isn't it? You found it with Kate and Simon.'

'Yeah.'

'I knew it would be something good.'

We climbed into the cave. I kept the torch pointing down with my back to Mum to stop him seeing her. I didn't want to see her either.

'Oooooo!' he cried. His voice echoed weirdly. He laughed and did it again. 'Have you explored everywhere in here?'

'It doesn't go anywhere. Come on now!'

'A bit further!' He pushed past, pulling me and peering into the gloom. 'There's a big mama rock!'

I was stunned. Had I heard right?

He tugged me over the slimy stones. He wasn't afraid at all. Letting go, he went right up to her.

She let him pat her cloak. 'Hello, Big Mama! How are you?'

I felt faint.

'What did she say?' I asked weakly.

He chuckled. 'Nothing. She's the silent type.'

Why had she let him recognise her? Was it some message to me? I'd have to think it out. I forced my

123

voice to sound normal. 'We've got to go now. You promised to be quick.'

'OK. We'll come back and see her another day, huh?'

'Maybe.' I shone the torch at the entrance to hurry him.

'Look, there's a bottle up there!' he said. Before I knew what was happening, he hurled a stone.

It missed the bottle, but whacked a rock wedged in the jumble above the tunnel. The rock moved. Then it was like I was magnum dizzy. Everything began shifting, sliding, falling.

I grabbed Arthur. I dragged him behind Mum. 'Get down!' I shouted over a rumbling like thunder. 'Duck your head!'

I threw myself across him, covering my own head with my arms. The cave was collapsing. With fearsome thuds, an avalanche of stuff hit the ground. I tensed, waiting for the rocks above to come down and mash us.

The cliff groaned. The crashing subsided to a shudder. Small stones fell, then a hiss of earth. It went deathly still.

Seized by a retching spasm of coughing, I sat up. My hand still clutched the torch. When I got enough breath, I rubbed the lens. The light shone into a swarm of dust motes.

Arthur was coughing too. 'What happened?' he wheezed, terrified.

'Your stone started a rock fall!'

'Stupid stone!' he spluttered.

Stupid kid, I wanted to scream. We had to get out of there! I jumped up. Grit slid off me. Clutching Arthur's

124

hand, I staggered around Mum to find the tunnel. We were doubled over with hacking.

Heaps of rubble lay strewn over the floor. Arthur stumbled beside me as I turned this way and that, trying to recognise something. I looked back at Mum's cloudy shape to get my bearings. The entrance must be behind a new slope at the front of the cave.

I climbed up the pile. Hunks of stone packed against the boulders of the cave wall. Not a crack of empty space. We were trapped!

'How we gonna get out?' wailed Arthur.

'Move the stones away from the opening, of course!' I shouted. I shoved the torch in my pocket and started shifting. We didn't have long. If we didn't get out fast, the tide would cut us off.

'There's a lot!' cried Arthur.

'So help!'

He clutched my waterproof. 'I didn't mean to make it all-fall-down,' he whimpered.

Poor little thing. Of course, he didn't. 'Don't worry,' I said, softening. 'We'll shift these.'

He smiled trustingly and picked up a rock. 'Big Mama protected us, didn't she?'

'Yeah,' I agreed. But I wasn't sure she meant to.

We wobbled up and down the rubble slope. It would have been quicker to throw the stones off, but I was scared we might start another rock fall.

When we stopped coughing, I dug in my pocket and held out a date. 'Something to give you energy.'

'Thanks, I'm hungry!' Arthur said. He wiped his mouth and eagerly popped it in. I had one too.

We cleared a layer. Then big stuff started to show. Rocks we couldn't budge in a million years. Supposing one of those was in front of the entrance? I didn't want Arthur to see them yet. I gave us both another date and set him to work at ground level.

Could the big rocks have come from the tunnel? I frantically heaved away everything I could from where the top of the slope met the cave wall. Perhaps the tunnel didn't exist anymore! I felt sick. A rescue team could get to us. Probably. With props or something, like when a coal mine collapses. But the cave would soon be cut off for hours. No one could look for us and guess we were inside.

Other sickening thoughts hit me. Why would anyone look here? I'd made sure Dad and Gilly didn't know about the cave, and Simon and Kate wouldn't expect me to bring Arthur. And what about my burglar trail? Maybe everyone would decide we'd been kidnapped.

Arthur screamed. He staggered backwards.

'What's the matter?' I clambered down.

A dark stain seeped from the base of the rocks.

## 22

I gaped. The tide was creeping in between the fallen rocks.

Arthur clung to me. 'It's coming to get us!'

'The sea always comes in here,' I said matter-of-factly. 'It won't get high.' Inside, my heart was thumping. The sea must have filled the channel already! We mustn't even try to move anything else until the tide went back out. But we couldn't stand in cold water for hours.

I glanced towards Mum. Would we get witched if we used her? I was frightened of getting that close. But there wasn't a choice.

'We'll climb up on Big Mama,' I said, taking Arthur's hand. I switched on the torch and led him through the rubble.

Forgetting what else was up there, I scraped fallen debris off her chest ledge. There was a bright flash as the necklace flew past. Arthur swooped on it.

'Gold! Pirate treasure!' He held it up, squinting. 'Gimme the torch.'

I didn't, but he realised what he had. 'It's Mummy's necklace! How did it get here?'

'I brought it. Come on, up there now.' I lifted him. He scrambled onto the ledge, gripping the necklace. I helped him turn and sit down.

'Why did you bring it?' he demanded.

I thought of saying I took it for a joke, but I was fed up with people pretending. 'I nicked it.'

'That was *mean*. She loves this.'

'Mind. I'm coming up.' I put the torch away and hoisted myself beside him.

'You and Mummy are always making each other sad.'

'Not sad. Mad. Because I won't take being bossed.'

'She cried yesterday.'

'To make Dad feel sorry for her.'

'And you were crying before I came.'

'Not about her.' My legs hung awkwardly over the narrow ledge. The stone rim dug into my thighs.

He went quiet.

Oh, what the heck. Let her have her precious loot. Mum didn't want it. 'Here, give me the stupid thing,' I said. 'I'll take it back.' If we get back.

He handed it over reluctantly. My hand trembled as I zipped it in the inside pocket of my waterproof. Of course we'd get back. We just had to wait. Eventually Simon and Kate would come and check the cave. But would it be after this high tide? It would be dark after the next one. And if rocks had fallen by the entrance, would they be able to tell where the cave was?

I had to stop thinking of awful possibilities. Just look after Arthur. I leaned back to make a comfortable place and held out my arms, but he didn't move closer. I popped my cheek with a finger.

'I hate it when you and Mummy fight,' he said.

128

'I know.'

A dark flush of wet spread through the rubble towards us.

'It's coming,' Arthur said in a small voice.

'Don't worry. We'll be OK up here. Big Mama's made of solid rock.' Pain welled up in me. I swallowed it, fighting the urge to cry.

'Is she stronger than my castle?'

'You bet. She's had the sea round her for years and years. Want another date?'

He took one, but his eyes stayed fixed on the scary water. 'How long will we have to sit here?'

'Just till the tide goes back out. Then we'll move the stones. A rescue party might come and help us from outside.' Please God!

I shone the torch on my watch. Quarter to eight. Gilly and Dad probably weren't even up yet!

When Arthur finished his date, he said, 'I'm thirsty.'

'Well, isn't it lucky I happen to have an apple?' Desperate for him to feel better, I handed it over.

He almost chucked the core. 'Don't throw anything!' I grabbed it and put it in a chink of rock. His hand felt freezing.

'You cold?'

He nodded. He had his fleece on. Better than a sweatshirt, but not enough.

'Put your hands in your pockets,' I said. I took off my waterproof. 'We'll share body heat. Explorers do that when they get lost on the mountainside.'

'We're not lost, are we? We're waiting for the tide to go out.'

'Right. See if you can tuck your legs under as well. I'll hold you.'

He nestled in. I arranged the waterproof over us both. We were friends again. He started sucking his thumb. I stroked his hair.

His breathing went slow and heavy. I rested my cheek on his head. I wanted to protect him. The feeling of loving him was so strong.

If I loved Arthur, how could a mother not love her own baby? *You must have loved me, Mum, under all the witched feelings.*

My eyelids drooped. My eyes opened and closed in the misty air. I drifted. In the centre of the mist, I became a tiny baby in my mum's arms. She was happy. I was happy. We were safe, cradled in a glow that filled the rocks and the vast sea and sky. The glow filled us too. I thought, of course we're safe. We're part of everything.

Pounding woke me from this blissful state. Icy cold nipped the back of my shoulders. My legs were numb.

I stared below my feet. We were surrounded with dark water. The pounding must be breakers smashing against the cliff outside.

I felt dizzy with fear. Arthur and I were sealed up in a cave, balanced above freezing seawater, and no one knew! I wanted to scream, shriek, howl, weep. But the dream left a little warm space of comfort inside and stopped me freaking out.

I shivered. Perhaps I was getting hypothermia. I circled my ankles. What if I got so numb I couldn't keep myself on the ledge?

Food would help. I didn't want to disturb Arthur by getting a date, so I inched a hand up for the apple core. I nibbled slowly, chewing till each bite became liquid, pips and all. It sounds disgusting eating someone else's apple core, but, honest truth, I felt grateful for every morsel.

Afterwards though, I realised I should have saved it. In fact, I was really stupid not saving the whole apple. We were going to be in here hours and hours. *Days* maybe!

I looked at my watch. Only eight thirty! When I tried to cover my shoulders, Arthur stirred.

'It's cold,' he whimpered.

I hugged him. 'Keep under the waterproof.' I prayed he wouldn't notice the water, but the cold made him restless. Soon he sat up straight. He gasped.

'It's *deep*!' His face twisted in panic. 'It's coming to smother us! I want Mummy!' He started to cry.

'The water doesn't get this high. There's a tidemark on the side of the cave.'

I shone the torch to try and find the mark to reassure him. The beam didn't reach, but I could see across to the wall. Was there more light in here now? I studied the roof. There was no sign of sky, but the gap was wider!

# 23

'The rocks have shifted up there,' I said to Arthur. 'I'm going to have a look.'

He dug his fingers into my arm. 'I want you to stay with me!'

'It'll only take a minute.' I wiped his tears. 'How about another date?'

He sniffed and nodded. When I rooted in the bag, I was horrified to find that there was only one left. But I couldn't take back the offer. He looked so scared.

I tucked the waterproof around him. 'Keep against the back of the ledge, OK?'

He nodded again, chewing, and staring at me out of big wet eyes. I kissed his nose. Then I carefully got my feet onto the ledge. When they took my weight, my legs went weak. Clinging to Mum, I stretched and shook them. They prickled painfully.

I put a foot on Mum's jutting chin. Help me, I begged. Don't break apart now.

I sprang and got both feet up. Then I straddled her nose, found a dip in her forehead, and finally pulled myself onto the top of her head.

Slowly, I stood up. I cautiously reached for the cave roof as I straightened. The last thing I wanted was to disturb anything loose. The rocks felt firm. I twisted and managed to squeeze through the gap as far as my shoulders.

The crashing of the sea echoed around a narrow, sloping vertical chamber. Light cut enticingly across rocks above. But I couldn't tell how safe they were. And I mustn't move Arthur unless there was a hope of getting out. I decided to lever into the chamber and investigate.

When I eased my arms through the gap, Arthur guessed that I was going higher. 'I'm coming with you!' he yelled.

'No, I'm only looking!' I squeezed back through the gap to explain and saw him grab Mum's chin. As he started to stand, the waterproof slipped off his shoulders.

'Aaaah!' he screamed in dismay.

The waterproof slid down the stone cloak and spread on the water. By the time I reached the ledge, it had drifted off and half sunk. I'd have to get in the water to fetch it, and it wouldn't be any use dripping wet. Neither would I.

I gulped. No food and no cover. If there wasn't a way out, we were definitely going to get hypothermia.

'I'm sorry!' Arthur wailed.

'It's OK. We're going to get out up there.'

'Can we?'

'Good chance. Think you can climb Big Mama?'

'Of course.'

'Let's feel your hands then.' One at a time, I held them under my sweatshirt and T-shirt against my skin. It warmed up my hands too.

'If anything moves while we're climbing, stop straight away,' I said.

133

'Don't want anymore all-fall-down, right?'

'Right.'

I fixed my arms each side of him as he climbed the face. There wasn't room on top of the head for both of us, and he was too little to reach the cave roof. I got as high as I could behind him.

'Get on my shoulders. Keep really still. *Really* still. I'm going to lift you to go through the gap first.' Geez, I wasn't sure if I was strong enough to do this without losing my balance.

But Arthur cheered up now we were back in action and moving away from the water. He confidently swung his leg over. 'The amazing aggro-bats, huh, Leslie?'

'You bet.'

I kneed onto the top of the head. Hard bits sliced my shins. I clung on like mad and got into a crouch. Oh help, Mum. Keep me steady.

'I'm going to stand up now. Grab the rocks and get your head through the space. Ready?'

'Go for it, go for it!'

My hands pushed off. I staggered a micro-step as I got up from my knees, but Arthur slapped his hands on the roof and gave us support. Bent over, I raised my arms over my head and clutched the rock too.

'It's light!' Arthur shouted.

'Can you climb up?'

'Yeah, yeah!' His trainers dug into my back. I kept quiet and gripped harder. At last, he was standing on my shoulders.

134

His weight lifted. I quickly pushed my head through into the chamber. Arthur was spread-eagled across the side of a sloping rock. I flinched, expecting him to slip, but he pulled himself higher into the sideways opening where the light came in. The chamber dimmed.

'What's it like?' I called.

'Titchy, but bright at the end.'

'Stop if anything moves!' This was so dangerous! Please, please, I prayed, don't let him get crushed!

I stood tiptoe on Mum's head. For a crazy moment, I was wrenched at leaving the cave. Then I hauled into the gap. When my feet were through, I pressed them against one side of the chamber and leaned my hands against the other.

At eye level, Arthur wiggled away between almost horizontal slabs. 'I'm a sandwich filling,' he called.

'What a batty filling!'

'I can see outside.'

'Is it big enough to get through?'

His feet disappeared. A bright patch shone at the end of the rocks.

'I'm out!' he yelled. 'Yay, yay, yay!'

He'd be on that steep cliff face. 'Wait for me!' I shouted. I squeezed between the slabs, edging forwards in a flat crawl.

I had to keep my head sideways, so I couldn't see the light any longer. Stone scraped my back. I was a thicker filling than Arthur. This is a jam sandwich, I joked to myself, trying to keep calm.

Then it wasn't funny. At all. The space got narrower. My chest hardly had room to breathe. I began to sweat. The rocks closed tight round me. I pushed, panic-stricken. I couldn't get any further.

Instinctively, I tried to pull back. But I couldn't move. I was wedged fast.

# 24

It was terrible, I mean it. Hard rock above. Hard rock below. Hard rock each side. Absolutely solid, uncaring, stupid rock.

I was clamped. I was suffocating.

My hair matted with sweat. My nose ran and made a sort of pool under my face. Inside my body, everything was dark. My mind struggled to get out. If I couldn't find a way to move, it would explode. My mind would splinter to fragments trapped in darkness forever.

It was so horrible I wanted to die to stop the feelings. I wanted to die like Mum. What did it matter if I died? I just caused trouble. No one would miss me.

Suddenly this incredible pack of understanding arrived in my head. How everyone was afraid they weren't good enough. That was why Gran and Dad worked so much. Why Dad was afraid of losing Gilly. Why Gilly was jealous of Mum and afraid of bad things happening. Why I was afraid Mum and Gilly didn't love me. Why Mum didn't stay.

It was crazy how we all hurt each other. People did the best they could, but things went wrong because they didn't trust the light that flowed through everything. Deep down we were the light, pure and clear and perfect. Deep down, everything was *all right*.

I was getting my wish to die. This was the last second

review. But now I didn't want to.

Even though there were difficult things, there was stuff like seagulls floating on angel wings, and Simon holding my hand, and Helen's music and Mum lifting spiders safe. Mum opening windows to let out wasps.

She wasn't sick then. She wanted them to live.

Then I knew Mum wasn't in the Big Mama rock. She was in me. Her caring true self was in me. Wanting me to live. Wanting me not to make the mistake she made. Wanting me to live for her too.

I heard Arthur shout. He sounded far away.

He must be climbing around. The stupid kid thought he could climb anything. 'Stay where you are!' I yelled.

I don't know if he heard. A stone rattled past. He screamed. 'It's slippery! *Leslie!*'

'*Stop moving about!*'

I had to get out there. I rammed forwards. I might as well get ripped open as rot in here after he fell.

Pain knifed back and front. My head buzzed from needing to breathe. I shoved again, determined to concentrate on the shoving not on the dark threatening from the corners of my mind. I jerked into a tighter clamp.

My fingernails scrabbled. My wrists strained. My toes pushed. And pushed.

Suddenly, my shoulders broke free. Another push and my head surfaced under open sky. A cloud drifted across. I breathed a gust of air. Fresh, light, floaty, delicious air. It was brilliant!

I wriggled out.

138

'Leslie!' Arthur squealed. He clung against earth and loose stones that seemed ready to make a landslide. I edged over and got an arm around his waist. He relaxed.

'Don't let go! I can't take your weight! I'll slip!'

We were a third of the way up the cliff. Below, the channel was gone. It was all heaving sea. Water bombs exploded against rocks, flinging shards of spray. Boulders hung as if they hadn't finished falling. The slab we had crawled along rested on them.

Above, between us and the sagging fence at the cliff top, rock edges and grass tuffs stuck out from scree and bare soil. Nowhere looked safe. But we were alive, and we had to stay that way.

A breaker crashed. A geyser shot up. Spray hit the back of our legs.

Arthur screamed. 'It's trying to bash us off!'

'We'll go higher. Don't look down.'

'I don't like climbing slidey stuff.'

Neither did I. But we couldn't hang on here. 'We're aggro-bats. We can't let the slidey stuff beat us. You were fantastic climbing out of the cave.'

Keeping hold of him, I tested higher up with the toe of my trainer. I found a slight edge and dug in. Then I helped him up beside me. Cautiously, I felt for another footrest.

It was slow. We kept slithering back. The wind worried at us, making it harder to hug the cliff. Vibrations from the hammering waves came up through the surface. Any minute one of us could somersault down to smash on the boulders, be tossed in the churning water.

Arthur killed. I choked at the terrible, terrible thought. It would wipe out Gilly. I didn't want revenge anymore. I didn't want to cause suffering to anybody.

We reached some grass clumps. I hoped we could use them for hanging on, but when I grabbed one, it threatened to come away. They were only good for keeping us steady as we struggled past.

Rain began to spit. If we got a downpour, we'd never be able to keep from slipping. A rim of rock jutted out of a bank of earth. Perhaps we could perch there while we waited for help.

I eased over and grasped it. The edge crumbled in my hand. My heart sank. What help was I expecting anyway? I checked the horizon. It was too rough for a boat to be near enough to spot us.

As I shifted to show Arthur where to put his foot next, I noticed ugly grubby thread ends hanging loose over the front of my sweatshirt. The beautiful embroidery was ruined. I bit my lip. It tasted of salt.

More and more, I had to support Arthur's weight. He was cold and tired. His teeth chattered. I saw that he was crying quietly.

'We're doing great. Not far now,' I urged. We had to keep moving. A drizzle was setting in.

But about three metres from the top, the slope got really steep. Much steeper than it had looked from below. We were practically upright against the cliff. Above was all rock.

I tugged Arthur up to a last clump of grass. He

slumped over it recklessly, limp as a rag doll. His cheeks were pale. His eyes were bloodshot.

'Can't go any further,' he whimpered.

'We're almost there!'

'Can't.'

I didn't know what to do. I felt exhausted. My feet were straining tiptoe on a stone sticking out among loose scree. The grass clump wasn't safe. The cliff top was close, but impossible. How could I get Arthur up sheer rock when he was knackered?

I leaned over him, sheltering him from the wind and the wet. Our faces made a little private space. 'I love you,' I whispered.

'I love you too,' he said.

Tears filled my eyes. I turned my head to look out at the big sea. Two seagulls sped by. Their shrieks mixed up with shouts.

# 25

'There, down there!'

I glanced up to the right. Simon and Gilly were charging through bushes behind the fence. Even at a distance, Gilly's eyes looked huge with alarm.

'HANG ON!' she shrieked. Talk about obvious, but was I glad to have her up there yelling it.

Arthur jerked back his head to see. I leaned in hard to stop him pitching us off the cliff. 'Mummy, Mummy!' he screamed.

Simon and Gilly leaned over the fence and gaped.

'*Flipping heck!*' said Simon.

'You're too far down to reach!' cried Gilly.

'Lower my jacket for them to hang on to,' said Simon, tearing it off.

'Mine's bigger!' cried Gilly. 'Hold up the wire. I'll lie flat underneath.'

They trampled around, pushing back gorse. My footrest was wobbling. I cautiously nudged each side of it, but couldn't find a firmer place.

Gilly's head appeared at the rock edge. She dangled her jacket by a sleeve. The other sleeve swayed above us. I seized it.

'Don't move!' Gilly ordered. 'Simon will run to the phone box and call the coastguard.'

We couldn't wait for that. But I mustn't panic Arthur.

'No, it's slippery,' I said. 'Arthur might be able to get high enough for you to pull him up.'

'I'm too tired!' he wailed. 'You get me, Mummy!'

'I would if I could, lovie!' she cried.

I knew she thought it was too dangerous to try to lift him without proper tackle. She had to understand! I stared straight at her, willing her to realise we were within seconds of falling.

Gilly met my eyes. Holding them, I said to Arthur, 'Mummy and I will help you.'

I never referred to her as Mummy for him. I saw her jolt as she got the message.

'That's right,' she said. Her voice shook. 'We'll help you.'

'I can't,' Arthur whimpered.

'If you climb onto this bit of grass, you'll be able to hold Mummy's jacket,' I urged.

'Please, lovie,' Gilly begged. She looked frantic.

Simon called, 'You can do it, aggro-bat!'

'The best act ever,' I said.

Arthur sighed. Determination set on his weary little face.

He struggled to get his knees on the clump. Its roots loosened. Soil came away and skittered down me. I leaned hard against the grass, hoisting Arthur up at the same time.

'I'll hold your legs,' Simon told Gilly.

Arthur grasped the jacket sleeve. I wrapped the end round one of his palms, closed the hand into a fist and put his other hand on the sleeve above.

'Well done, well done!' Gilly gabbled desperately. 'Hang on tight now, lovie. Stand up carefully. Don't let go when the jacket moves. You'll need to use your feet, but it won't be far before I can reach you. Leslie's helping. Don't forget to use your feet. Don't let go, whatever you do!'

She was confusing him.

'I'm going to push and Mummy's going to pull,' I said.

He clambered upright. I pressed in harder. The stone under me drooped.

'Here we go,' I said. 'Like climbing Big Mama. First foot up.' He raised it, but got no leverage on the wet rock. It slid back. I pushed his behind as he tried again. Gilly lifted, but I had to keep supporting him. He didn't have the strength to hold the jacket on his own.

'Bit higher, bit higher,' Gilly yattered. 'Make your feet help. Not much further. Don't let go!'

She almost had him. My footrest tilted. I pushed full stretch the second before it gave. Gilly clamped his wrists. 'Got you!'

The stone dropped from under me as she went on wittering. I grabbed the hummock. It came away. I flung myself against the cliff. I skidded, but no one saw.

My fingers scuffed through stones and damp earth. Gravel grazed my nose. I clasped an edge of rock and clung dizzily.

It sounded like Arthur was getting to the top. I heard Simon cheer. Gilly ordered, 'Bend the wire more!'

I must keep quiet till they had him safe. The pounding of the waves went through me like my own pulse. If I moved a fraction, I'd be down there with them. I pressed into the cliff like I was part of it. I remembered the light that goes through everything. I remembered Mum was in me, wanting me to live.

Then Simon yelled, 'Leslie's slipped!'

Gilly screamed. 'Hold on, hold on!' she shrieked. 'Give me that jacket! Quick!'

Couldn't the idiot see I was too far down to reach it now? My only hope was rescue people with ropes. But it would be a million years before they came.

I heard mumbling and scuffling. Simon said, 'Are you sure?' and Gilly cried, 'She'll FALL! Arthur, get right away!'

I studied the grit beside my cheek. A small purplish stone shone in the rain. Crazily, I wanted to shout that I'd found a piece of jasper.

Something brushed my hair. Simon yelled, 'The jacket's on your right, Leslie!'

How could it be? Straining to keep the rest of me fixed, I groped. Incredibly, I touched fabric. I clutched it and glanced up.

Simon and Gilly's jackets were knotted together. They were tied to Gilly's ankle! Somehow she was hanging down the rock face. 'Quick as you can!' she yelled.

She didn't need to tell me. I hauled myself upwards, digging in my trainers where I could. I prayed the jackets and her famous non-slip knots would hold.

'Grab my legs,' she said breathlessly when I got to where her feet pushed into the cliff. 'Use me to climb.'

I realised she was hanging on to the metal fence post. Her arms must be ready to snap. 'Can you take my weight?'

'*Yes, yes!*'

I heaved on up, one hand clinging to her and the other scrabbling for a grip on the rock. Her head twisted at an awkward angle to watch how I did. She frowned with concentration. She had the same determined look as Arthur.

'Way to go!' encouraged Simon. He was anchored behind the fence post. I had a quick glimpse of his hands each side, clasping Gilly's wrists.

'Don't you lean over!' Gilly shouted at him.

My hand clawed the edge. Simon grabbed it. Keeping one arm around the post, he pulled. I let go of Gilly. He dragged me under the wire. Gasping, I crawled through a spiky mash of gorse out of the way while he helped Gilly.

Arthur flung his arms around my neck. Then Gilly and Simon were there too in one big scrum. Gilly was hugging me and Arthur. She squashed us together, panting, 'Thank God! Thank God!'

Simon leaned through the huddle. And covered in dirt, two centimetres from my family, full on the lips, I got my first kiss.

## 26

When Gilly untied her jacket from her ankle, the ghastly realisation hit me. My waterproof was left buried in the cliff, and in its pocket was her necklace.

'We had to get out of a cave, Mummy!' cried Arthur. 'It all-fell-down when I threw a stone. Water came in!'

I exchanged a look with Simon and guessed they had come this way because he'd thought of the cave.

Gilly gripped her head. 'What were you *doing* in a cave? Why did you go out without telling me?'

'You were asleep,' whimpered Arthur. 'I followed Leslie. She didn't want me to go in the cave.'

'Oh, lovie!'

Gilly glanced at me. I saw her take in my ruined sweatshirt. She jumped up. 'We must get back! We've been out of our minds! Daddy could be phoning the police by now. He was going to drive around the lanes. Helen and Kate went along the cliff path.'

No one seemed to have noticed the burglar trail. When Gilly couldn't find us, she'd run to the beach. Then she banged up Simon's family and got everyone searching.

'My turn to give you a piggyback,' Simon said to Arthur.

Arthur clung to Gilly. 'I want Mummy to carry me!'

'Mummy's arms are tired,' said Simon, lifting him off her. Arthur let him.

We had to go single file between the bushes and brambles, so Gilly couldn't cross-examine me. She went behind Simon with her hand on Arthur's back. I staggered after them through the drizzle, feeling as if I were sleepwalking.

When we were almost at the fence, Dad ran down the track. He rushed to the fence, catching his breath in gulps. 'You're all right!'

He leaned across and took Arthur from Simon. Arthur buried his face in Dad's shoulder.

'They were stranded on the rocks!' Gilly announced dramatically. 'Trapped in a cave first!'

Dad looked at me with despair. 'Couldn't you see the tide coming?' he shouted.

Simon swung a leg over the fence. He helped me climb. Gilly pushed up on my elbow.

'I'll go and find Mum and Kate,' Simon said.

'Thank them so much!' Gilly gushed. 'And thank *you*!'

Simon hopped to the ground and held my waist. My knees gave as I jumped down.

He steadied me. 'You're zonked!'

I felt miserable. What a mess I'd made of our last day! At the cottage, I went straight to my room. I got up the stairs by leaning on my hands. I pulled off my filthy jeans and ripped sweatshirt, crawled under both duvets, and sobbed.

Yes, Arthur had followed me, but it was my *going* that got us into danger. It was my fault we almost got killed.

And any minute Dad and Gilly would find out about the necklace.

There was tap on the door. Gilly came in with a mug. 'Have some milky cocoa.'

Arthur must not have told her. Well, he wouldn't, would he? Poor little kid, always caught in the middle. Always trying to stop us from fighting.

Gilly squatted beside me with the steaming cocoa. I wanted its warmth and sweetness, but I couldn't stop crying. She put the mug on the floor by my clothes heap and handed me some tissues. I waited for her to tell me off for wrecking the sweatshirt. Also for getting into bed without washing.

'I understand why you wanted to run off,' she said. 'I'm sorry I hit you yesterday.' Gilly apologising! I couldn't believe my ears.

'Arthur says you found a way out of the cave when the sea came in. And you got him up that terrible cliff – oh, I can hardly *bear* to think of it! You've been so brave. You've been wonderful.'

I sobbed harder. Wait till she knew!

'You're probably in shock,' she said.

'No! I've done something awful!' I had to get it out. 'I took your necklace.'

Her hand went to her bare throat. 'What do you mean?'

'I stole it. It's left in my waterproof in the cave.'

She sat back on the floor, looking in shock herself.

'I'm sorry,' I cried. 'It was horrible of me! But I don't

149

think I can get it. Or the waterproof. I almost got stuck where we got out.' Heaving sobs took over as I remembered the blackness.

'Don't even think of going back in!' Gilly gasped. 'Promise me you won't!'

I nodded. I knew I absolutely couldn't, ever.

We looked straight into each other's eyes for the second time that day, perhaps for the second time in our lives.

'I've done lots of things wrong as well,' she said. She blinked. Her eyelashes were wet. 'I got it wrong from the start with us, didn't I?'

Her eyes moved to Mum's photo on the chest of drawers. 'Your dad says you've been asking about her.' She was having trouble speaking. 'I've been thinking about her too. How – sad it is for you and your dad – to have lost her.'

I didn't know what to say.

'In the beginning, I thought I could take her place,' said Gilly. 'I rushed in all gung-ho and got rid of Shushy. I thought she was getting you into bad habits. And, well, more than that, *I* wanted to be the one you depended on. But it seemed as if you were angry at me for not being your birth mother. So I got angry, because it wasn't my fault. Because I was trying hard. Because *I would have liked to have been your birth mother*!'

We stared at each other. I think we were both startled by what she had said. After a silence, I blew my nose and she handed me the cocoa. 'Are you warm enough? I'm sorry the central heating doesn't work.'

150

'It's OK. Arthur brought me an extra duvet.' I lifted it to show her. 'Is he all right?'

'Sound asleep on the sofa. You *were* wonderful looking after him. The necklace can go. We've got the two of you back safe!'

After she went downstairs, I drank the cocoa. I thought about Gilly, and I thought about Mum, and I thought about Simon saying *This is how it is*.

I touched Mum's photo. I felt grateful I'd found that little warm place inside where I hadn't lost her. It was snuggled in the empty hurting hole I used to have. The hole wasn't all healed up, but it felt better.

I lay down and went to sleep.

# 27

Everyone was on the beach for our final morning. Arthur kept telling about the humungous all-fall-down.

'I did it! Not the sea!' he repeated about fifty times. Probably stopped it feeling so scary.

When I saw Kate juggling pebbles, I decided to make the collection Gilly wanted. Once I started, I really got into it. The others did too. People kept shouting, 'Have we got this one?' and showing Simon or running to identify it in the book.

At breakfast, I'd told Gilly, I'd save to buy her another gold necklace. I planned to use presents and my pocket money after the oar was paid for. I also hoped to find a way to earn some cash.

Gilly said, 'I don't want you to do that. But thanks for offering, Leslie.' Her calm tone made me feel she meant it.

Dad smiled shyly at us. Before we came down to the beach, he gave me a hug.

We laid the pebble collection on the blanket. 'Shall we record them in the back of the book?' asked Gilly.

'Yeah, good idea,' I said.

'I've got a pen,' said Dad. He dug it out with his usual revved-up enthusiasm.

'O-*K*,' said Kate. 'How many of these do you remember, Mum?'

'Limestone, quartz – uh...' Helen started laughing.

'Granite,' said Gilly, eagerly taking over. 'Serpentine, sandstone, slate.'

Simon and I drifted away. He gave me a twinkly grin. 'Let's see if there are any interesting ones stuck between the rocks.'

We climbed over the boulders the tide hadn't reached. Simon crouched in a gulley. 'Here!'

I got down beside him.

He said, 'Would you like to come and stay for a weekend when Mum gets back from the concert tour?' He looked away for a nanosecond like he *still* wasn't one hundred per cent certain I adored being with him.

'I'd love to!' I said. And I kissed him. And he kissed me back. And he got closer and kissed me again.

And then Arthur's head appeared over a rock. 'Leslie and Simon are smoochy-cooching!' he yelled.

'Hey, you!' said Simon.

We jumped down onto the shingle. Gilly and Dad glanced up and smiled at each other. It seemed a sharing sort of smile, not a ready-to-tease one. It reminded me of the old couple on the bench at the headland. I felt a flicker of gladness that Dad had Gilly.

We played water tag again. Gilly didn't try to coax Arthur in. She must have believed me about the lessons, because he said they were finished.

I decided that later on I'd ask if he'd like to come and mess around at the swimming pool with me. Perhaps while Gilly was learning the violin for herself. She was fizzing to start since Helen convinced her it wasn't too late.

I see now that Dad's right about Gilly and me both being strong-willed. What I have to try is not to get wound up when we disagree. It doesn't feel good when I lose my cool.

One thing that helps is remembering climbing the cliff. It hit me that on that cliff I climbed someone acting like a real mother. Someone who risked her life for me. Since that time, I've known Gilly cares about me.

She cares a lot.

# RUTH DOWLEY

Rosamund and Sam look forward to living at the medieval manor house bought by their new stepfather, Richard. But Richard soon takes a dislike to Sam and becomes over familiar with Rosamund. Her room is reputed to be haunted by another Rosamund, who lived there in Tudor times. As Rosamund faces an increasing threat of sexual abuse, it is the parallel struggle of the first Rosamund that helps her believe no one has the right to take over her body and mind.

'The book deals sensitively with the difficult subiect of sexual abuse...a compelling and insightful read.'

*Achuka* Children's Books UK

ISBN 0 86264 338 4  £4.99